Clara Mulholland

Percy's revenge

a story for boys

Clara Mulholland

Percy's revenge
a story for boys

ISBN/EAN: 9783337414313

Printed in Europe, USA, Canada, Australia, Japan

Cover: Foto ©Andreas Hilbeck / pixelio.de

More available books at **www.hansebooks.com**

PERCY'S REVENGE:

A STORY FOR BOYS.

BY

CLARA MULHOLLAND.

BOSTON:
THOMAS B. NOONAN & CO.
17, 19 AND 21 BOYLSTON ST.
1887.

CONTENTS.

PERCY'S REVENGE.

CHAPTER I.

HUGH BROWN'S HOME.

"MOTHER, mother, I've got the prize. Hurra! Hurra! I am a lucky chap," cried Hugh Brown, as he dashed noisily into the parlor where his mother sat at work.

"Gently, dear Hugh, or you will wake poor Susie, and she has not been very well all day," said Mrs. Brown, in a whisper. "But show me your prize, dear. I am very glad you have won it." And drawing the eager boy to her side, she kissed him tenderly.

"There was such fun at school to-day, mother," he said, glancing at the cot wherein his little sister lay, and lowering his voice. "As it was an extra prize given for holiday work, there was great excitement over it, and when my name was called out, the fellows cheered and shouted tremendously. Mr. Smith said I had worked well, and that I was the best pupil he had."

"I am quite sure of that, Hugh."

"Well, you see, mother, I want to get on as fast as ever I can to help you and father. But some of the fellows were very jealous and disagreeable about it. Harry Jones turned up his nose, and said he was just as clever as I was, and he could have got the prize if he had wanted to, only he didn't work for it."

"But why didn't he?"

"Oh, he was in the country, he said, and he wasn't going to spend his holidays stewing over Latin verses. But"—

"My poor Hugh, I wish you had been in the country," said his mother, sadly. "These hot summer months in London, and the long hours you spent over your work, have made you pale and thin."

"Not a bit of it, mother mine. Don't you go fretting about me, for I'm as well as possible. I feel so glad about my prize," and Hugh hugged his big book lovingly.

"Yes, dearest, so am I, and I am sure your father will be delighted."

"That he will," cried Hugh, brightly. "But, mother, why is father so late? I was sure he would have been at home. He is not generally out at this hour."

"No; and I cannot think what is keeping him. He expected to be back by five o'clock. He went into the city on business, Hugh."

"Into the city?" said Hugh, quickly. "Is he really going to take to an office again? Poor father, it will be hard on him."

"Yes, he will feel it greatly, for he cannot bear the drudgery of office work," said Mrs. Brown, sighing. "But something must be done. No publisher will buy his books and stories, and we have only a few pounds left to live upon. If he does not get this place that he has gone to see about, we must fall very low, indeed."

"How I wish I was old enough to work. Then father could sit at home and write his books in peace, and you could make pretty frocks for Susie, instead of those horrid shirts that blind your eyes, and bring you in so little money."

"Very little, dear, but I am thankful to be able to earn it."

"Of course; I know you are. But supposing I were a merchant or a barrister earning heaps and heaps of money, you wouldn't think much of it, I can tell you. I'd bring you home every penny, and you might just do what you liked with it. Wouldn't that be jolly, mother mine?"

"Delightful, dearest. But my Hugh must grow big and strong, and learn a great many things before he can hope to earn any money. Boys of thirteen can only study well, be good and obedient, and so prepare themselves to be clever, industrious men."

"Yes, I know; but it does take a fellow so long to grow up—at least when he's longing, longing to help his mother."

"So it does, dear. But you do help your mother, Hugh, in more ways than you imagine."

"Do I, mother? I am so glad. But still I should like to earn money for you."

"And so you shall, some day. Meanwhile, my Hugh must be patient, and do the work that lies before him—the work that God wishes him to do. If your father gets this situation in the city and keeps it, I shall be truly thankful and able to manage nicely."

"Oh, I hope he may get it. I am sure he will," cried Hugh with a loving kiss. "And now I think I'll run down to the door and wait till I see father come up the street. I want to be the first to tell him the good news about my prize. And, mother, if he has got that place, I'll just give a cheer on the stairs, and then you'll know."

"No, dear, please do not mind cheering. You might wake Susie."

"Of course. What a duffer I am. Well, you will soon know when you see our faces. I'll grin from ear to ear with joy if it's all right. Dear little Susican, as if I would wake you, even with good news," he whispered; and running to the cot, he gazed fondly down on the little sleeper, a delicate-looking child of four years old. "Mother, when I grow big and earn all that money, we'll take Susie to the country. That will bring the roses to her cheeks. But ta-ta, I must not build any more castles in the air. '*Au reservoir*,' as Lord Tom Noddy says," and taking up his cap, Hugh ran out of the room, and down the stairs, singing merrily as he went.

"That prize has turned the boy's head, I think," said his mother, with a smile, and glancing anxiously at the cot. But Susie still slept peacefully, quite undisturbed by her brother's noisy exit; so Mrs. Brown poked the fire, trimmed her lamp, and applied herself diligently to her shirt-making.

And now, as the poor lady bends patiently over her work, I will tell my readers, in as few words as possible, the history of this little family. Some fourteen or fifteen years before the beginning of this story, a foolish young couple resolved to get married in spite of the strong opposition of their friends.

Philip Brown was a young man of literary tastes and some ability; but, who, work as he would, found it very hard to live upon what he made by his pen. And as the girl he wished to make his wife was the child of rich parents, the match was considered most unsuitable. But the young people were self-willed, and, taking matters into their own hands, got married without waiting for any one's permission.

Philip's friends were few and poor, and could do nothing to help him. His wife's father was very wealthy; but so angry was he with her, that he refused to have anything to do with her, and never saw her again. She had chosen to disobey him, she must suffer for her disobedience.

But, at last, hearing melancholy accounts of the wretched condition to which the young people were reduced, he offered to give them a certain sum of money, if they would go to Australia, and never trouble him more. This they gladly agreed to do, and in a short time the husband and wife were on their way to the Bush.

There they remained for several years, and although their life was a hard one, yet it was fairly happy. There little Hugh was born; and as he grew up strong and healthy, he brought joy and happiness into the lonely cottage.

But when Hugh was nine years old, a sudden change came in their lives.

Without any apparent cause, Philip grew restless; declared himself weary of the wild life in the bush, and giving up his work there, went off to Melbourne, where he obtained a situation as clerk in a bank.

Poor Mrs. Brown was pained by this strange conduct; but finding it useless to remonstrate, she settled down as cheerfully as she could, and tried to make the best of everything.

Then poor little delicate Susie was born, and the mother longed for the fresh country air to bring the roses to her darling's cheeks. But her husband seemed. happy in the town, and she strove to be content.

But soon Philip became dissatisfied once more, and throwing up his situation, hurried his wife and children off to London, where he established them in shabby lodgings in a small street off Tavistock Square.

Why her husband made this move and spent so much of their hard-earned savings on such a useless journey, Mrs. Brown could not understand. He gave her no explanation of his conduct, telling her simply that they were to return to England, as he found it dreary work living in Australia.

And when they reached London, to her surprise and alarm, he sought for no employment.

In Melbourne he had worked in a bank, and earned sufficient for their daily wants; but here he shut himself up in the house from morning till night writing.

"Philip," said his wife, "our money is almost gone. What shall we do when it is spent?"

"Do not be alarmed, little woman," he answered, pointing to a pile of manuscript. "There is something that will make our fortune. I have written a book, dear, and when it is published you and I shall be rich. So do not fret about money."

But Mrs. Brown could not help fretting, as month after month passed away, and her purse became lighter and lighter.

The book had been finished and sent from one publisher to another; but, alas, without success. It was always declined " with thanks," and there was no money forthcoming to keep the family from want.

Then, at last, Mrs. Brown implored her husband to look for some employment by which he could earn bread for his children.

Disappointed and disgusted at the failure of his book, Philip did as she desired. But his heart was not in his work; he was careless and inattentive, and soon received notice to leave the office.

Again he tried to write a successful book; again failed, and once more went out in search of a situation.

This he was fortunate enough to obtain; and, had he been hard-working and steadfast, all would have been well. But he was neither, and was always dreaming of the great things he might do with his pen.

At the end of the second year, a short tale

was published in a magazine; and, wild with excitement, he again threw up his situation; and, telling his wife that he was now certain to get on, buried himself in his papers.

But, alas, success was as far off as ever; and after plodding for many months at a book, and suffering many bitter disappointments in having it returned to him, he flung it aside; and vowing that he would never write another story, went off to the city to answer an advertisement that he had seen in the *Times*.

"Poor Philip," said Mrs. Brown, with a sigh, as she pondered over the sad story of her life, " God grant that you may get this place and keep it. The money we got for our little place in Australia is all but gone. What I earn by my shirt-making is very, very small; and unless something is done, I know not what may happen. Poor fellow, would that you were more steadfast, more plodding. How much better is it to work on at one thing, even if the pay is small, than to strain after something great but uncertain. Patience and perseverance are truly virtues that every one should cultivate. I hope and trust that my bright Hugh may possess them. Then, indeed, he will be a comfort to me. But, my goodness, what can that noise be?" she exclaimed, as the sound of heavy tramping feet was heard coming up the stairs. "What can they be bringing up?"

At this moment the door opened, and Hugh crept into the room, looking startled and afraid.

"Mother, mother, it's"—he began. But he seemed choking and the words refused to come.

"It's what, child? Who is tramping up the stairs? Why, Hugh, you look like a ghost. Let me go and see what is the matter."

"Mother, darling," whispered the boy, "It's father. They say he's not dead—but—oh!—he looks so white and strange."

"Looks white and strange—but is not dead. What do you mean, Hugh? Why do you talk in such a manner?" she cried, trembling with fear.

"Mother—he is ill—he"—

"Where child—where is your father? Where"—

"Here—here I am, dear. But don't be frightened, Lucy," said Philip, in a weak voice, as he came in, leaning on an old man's arm. "I fainted at the foot of the stairs, and the boy was startled."

"Philip, Philip, what has happened? You who were always so strong?" cried the poor woman, throwing herself on her knees beside him, as he lay panting on the sofa.

"It isn't much, darling," he whispered, "but this weakened me;" and as he removed the handkerchief that he held to his mouth, she saw, with horror, that it was covered with blood.

"Please, ma'am, an' I think he didn't ought to talk," said the old man who had helped him home. "Put him to bed, an' make him as comfortable as you can, an' he'll be all right to-morrow, I'm thinkin'. It was in Oxford Street it happened, just as he was goin' across. A big omnibus knocked him down, an' made him turn weak like. I jumped from my old cart, an' pulled him on to the pavement. When he came to, the policeman was for puttin' him in a cab, but he seemed agin' it like, so I just put him in my cart an' brought him where he telled me he lived. But, Lor' love ye, there's people gets run over every day a'most, an' they're none the worse for it. Put him in bed, ma'am, an' he'll be all right to-morrow. He's just a bit shaken, an', as he says, the bleedin' made him weak like."

But the unhappy wife was too terrified to take any comfort from his words, and gazed at him in a startled manner, as if she did not understand. So, seeing that he could do nothing to help her, the old man bade her "good-night," passed out of the room and down the stairs, sighing as he went.

"Do not fret, Lucy dear, do not fret," whispered Philip, as his wife sat weeping by his bedside some few hours later; "you have made me nice and comfortable, and, please God, I'll soon be well again."

But the next morning he was so weak and ill that it was quite impossible for him to get up, and his wife and children were filled with sorrow as they watched the pale, sad face, that they had known so bright and healthy. He himself kept wonderfully brave, and, in spite of his own misgivings, did what he could to raise their drooping spirits.

"Never mind, dear," he said, with a faint smile, and kissing little Susie, who nestled close to his side, "I must just rest for a few days, and then when this queer pain goes away, I'll be as strong as ever. I did not get that situation, Lucy, but I heard of another much better. When I get over the effects of this shock, I'll go and see about it. I am sure to get it, I think. So don't be down-hearted, dear wife, but try and look cheerful, like this sweet child and me."

But Mrs. Brown did not feel satisfied and sent Hugh off for the doctor, as she was anxious to know if her husband had been seriously injured by his accident. The doctor came and examined him carefully; he asked him to cough, felt his pulse, and then told him gently to keep very quiet. The unhappy wife followed the doctor down the stairs; and as time went on, and she did not return, Philip grew restless and uneasy. Hugh did what he could to soothe him; but, at last, finding this difficult, he ran out of the room to look for his mother. Sitting on the stairs, her face bathed in tears, her whole frame shaken with sobs of bitter anguish, was poor Mrs. Brown.

"Hugh, Hugh," she cried, pressing the boy in her arms. "It makes me wild with grief to see your father so ill — so weak. But do not let him know that I am weeping. The doctor says we must keep him cheerful, so don't cry my little man. Go in again and tell him I have gone to get him some medicine."

Very bravely Hugh choked back the tears

that came into his eyes at the sight of his beloved mother's grief; and trying hard to look
bright and pleasant, returned to his father's
room.

Little Susie had fallen asleep, her curly head
resting comfortably on the sick man's breast;
so the boy delivered his mother's message in a
whisper, and sat down by the bedside.

" Read to me, Hugh," said his father. " It
will help to pass the time for me, and Susie
will not hear you. She is too fast asleep to be
easily disturbed."

" Yes, father, with great pleasure," said
Hugh, and taking down his prize, a richly
bound copy of the New Testament, he began
to read in a clear, distinct voice. The sick man
turned his eyes with delight upon his son, and
listened attentively to the beautiful and consol-
ing words.

When Mrs. Brown returned with the medicine, all traces of sorrow had disappeared, and
she spoke so cheerfully that both Philip and
and Hugh were reassured by her manner, and
did not realize the silent agony she was enduring.

The doctor came every day, and Mrs. Brown
looked out eagerly for his coming. But alas !

his visits did not comfort her, for long and bitter were the fits of weeping that came upon her after he went away.

Days and weeks passed over. The doctor came and went; but Philip still lay on his sick bed; and the poor woman's heart sank low, as she saw starvation and want staring her in the face. Long and earnest were her prayers to God, for she found it hard to resign herself without bitterness to his holy will. But she struggled bravely, and tried her best to be humble and submissive.

Every moment she could spare, from attendance on the sick man, was devoted to needlework; but the little she could earn in this way was not enough to keep her family from want. In all London she had not a friend to whom she could go for aid; and she knew not what to do.

Hugh had left school and did all he could to help his mother; but his face wore a sad look that pierced the poor woman's heart, as she thought of all his dreams for the future shattered and gone forever.

"My poor Hugh; my bright, clever boy," she murmured. "To think what you might have been, and what you must be now, since I can no longer keep you at school. And my little Susie, with her sweet, delicate face, must I take her to the workhouse or allow her to die of starvation? Oh, father, were you alive I would go to you, brave your anger, and implore your assistance for my unhappy family. But alas! you are dead; you, my mother — my only sister — all dead, and there is not a soul to whom I could go in my dire distress. My God, my God, have mercy on me and mine," and bowing her head upon the table before her, she wept aloud in her anguish.

How long she remained in this position she never knew; but, as she sat, she felt a pair of arms round her neck, a little cheek against her own, and Hugh whispered joyfully in her ear:

" Look up mother, and don't cry any more, I have thought of a plan — a fine plan — and I am going to earn heaps of money for you and father. I am, indeed, and I am going to begin to-morrow."

# CHAPTER II.

HUGH BEGINS TO WORK.

THE next morning, as the clock struck four, Hugh tumbled out of bed, and, lifting the curtain that hung before his window, peeped out.

It was a regular November morning, wet, foggy, and cold. But this seemed to please our young friend immensely, for he cut capers of delight when he saw the state of the weather.

"The very thing," he cried. "A right down jolly sort of a day for what I want," and he dressed himself quickly, whistling gayly as he donned a much-patched, shabby-looking suit. Then kneeling by his bedside, he clasped his hands devoutly, and raising his blue eyes to heaven, begged God to bless and help him in this work that he was about to undertake for the sake of his sick father and suffering mother.

Then, feeling strong and courageous, he slipped down to the little sitting-room, where he found his mother ready to give him his breakfast.

" What do you think of me, mother dear?" he asked, with a merry laugh, as he kissed her, and bade her good-morning. " Don't I look ' spiffing,' as Jack Martin says?"

" Indeed, you look very shabby, dear Hugh," said his mother, sadly. " And I cannot bear to see you start off on such a foolish errand. It is a dreadful morning, dear, so just stay where you are."

" A dreadful morning is exactly what I want, mother dear; for if it was fine I might as well stay at home," he answered gayly. "A sunny day would ruin me. So you ought to be glad to see the rain."

" My poor boy, how could I be glad?" she cried, with tears in her eyes. " Why, it almost kills me to think of my son starting off in the drenching rain to take to such work — such low, degrading work."

" Now, mother dear, don't think of it that way. It's the only work that I can do just at present, so don't try to turn me from it. I've had a fine breakfast, and this coat is warm, although it is a little patched."

" My poor lad, you have a brave heart, and God will bless you for doing your best," she said, with a kiss. " You are a great comfort to me, Hugh, in this time of terrible trouble."

" That is grand news, mother dear, and makes me happier than anything I have heard for a long time. And now, keep up your spirits, for if I can earn a little money, just to help us to keep things going, till father is able to go after that situation, it will be a jolly good thing, and won't do me a bit of harm. Good-by, mother; I must be off."

Then he kissed her long and lovingly, took up a little broom that stood ready in the corner, and putting on an old, tattered cap, sprang lightly down the stairs.

It was bitterly cold, and Hugh shivered and coughed, as the thick, yellow fog went down his throat.

" Poor mother was right. It is a bad morning to be out. But if I can just do what I want and earn a little money to take home, I shan't mind how disagreeable it is. It is a right good thing I thought of this kind of work, for it is easy enough, and pretty certain even if it is unpleasant;" and drawing his jacket more tightly round him, he splashed bravely through the mud.

On and on went Hugh, up one street and down another, looking out anxiously for a crossing that required sweeping. But at every corner he found a man or woman, armed like himself, with a good stout broom. This was a state of affairs he had not counted upon; and, as the morning wore on, his hopes of earning any money gradually vanished. So, feeling weary and disheartened, he leaned against a shop window and began to cry.

He had wandered several miles from home, and was now in the busy Strand. There was plenty of mud and many crossings to be swept; but, alas, for Hugh, there were crowds of sweepers, and not a spot for him and his little broom.

As he stood gazing about him in silent despair, his eye fell upon a hobbling old man, who knocked the mud about in a lazy fashion and grumbled audibly when an occasional copper was thrown to him by a passer-by. He was a sour-faced fellow, and Hugh noticed that few persons gave him anything, whilst many

shuddered and hurried away when he spoke
to them.

"That's a queer-looking old man," thought
Hugh. "But he's jolly lucky to have found a
crossing to sweep. I wish I could get one,"
and sighing heavily, he turned away his
head.

"Well, young un. What are yer after?"
and, turning round, Hugh saw the old crossing-
sweeper peering at him from under two bushy
eyebrows.

"I'm after work," replied Hugh, growing
very red. "But there doesn't seem to be
much to do about here at least."

"Oh, there's plenty of work, but little pay,"
grumbled the old man. "But see 'ere now,
yers got a hinnocent face, an' that allus pays.
So, I'll give yer my place on the crossin', if
yer'll give me 'arf of all yer gets to-day.'

"Very well," answered Hugh. "But I'm
afraid that won't be much, for, there doesn't
seem to be much money going about. However, I may as well work, when I get the
chance, so here goes."

"I'll keep my heye on yer, my fine cove,"
cried the old fellow. "I'll watch every penny
yer gets; but, first of all, I must go in an' get

a drop o' gin to warm myself;" and off he hobbled, leaving Hugh master of the crossing.

For many hours, the poor boy remained at his post, working and sweeping, but without much profit.

The rain fell in torrents, and few persons were out, except those who were hurrying to their work, and they, poor souls, had not many pence to throw to the crossing-sweepers. The old man did not return from warming himself, and Hugh felt a great desire to throw down his broom and go after him. But the thought of his sick father and anxious mother kept him to his work, and he continued his sweeping, hoping and praying that some kind, well-to-do persons might soon pass by.

And presently the heavy rain ceased; the thick fog cleared away and a pale, sickly sun came struggling through the clouds. A great change soon took place in the streets. Carts, cabs, and carriages crowded the roads, and blocked up the crossings. Well-dressed, happy-looking people, stood watching an opportunity to cross, and many a kindly glance fell upon little Hugh, as he stood grasping his muddy broom in his frozen hands. Purses were drawn forth, money was quickly given, and the tired boy grew light-hearted and happy, as he heard the pennies rattling in his pocket.

At last the weary day drew to a close, and as darkness came on, Hugh felt that he might go home, and delight his mother with a sight of his riches.

But, suddenly, he remembered his promise to the surly old man, and he looked about to see where he could be.

" I promised him half, and he must get it," he said. "He looks cross and disagreeable, but he has been a true friend to me ; for where should I have gone if he had not given me his crossing? Where can he be, I wonder? I must just see how much I have to give him when he turns up."

So, talking away cheerfully to himself, in spite of cold and wind, Hugh managed to count his money, and found, to his delight, that he had five shillings.

Putting half of his little fortune in one pocket and the remaining half in the other, he was about to begin his search for his surly friend when a tall, handsome gentleman passed quickly over the crossing.

Drawing out his purse as he went along, he tossed something to Hugh, and disappeared.

Laughing merrily at this unexpected addition
to his wealth, the boy stooped to pick up, as
he thought, a penny, and found, to his amazement, a bright new sixpence.

"Threepence more for old Sour-Face," said
Hugh, gayly. "Why, if I hadn't to give him
some of the money I'd be quite rich. But,
never mind, I shan't give him any to-morrow,
and two and ninepence isn't bad for a beginning. But, where is the old boy? Holloa,
what on earth is that?"

As he stood swinging his broom to and fro
in the mud, it suddenly knocked against something hard, and, looking down, Hugh saw a
large, leather pocket-book, with silver corners,
and a raised monogram on one side. Picking
it up, he rubbed it with his sleeve; wondered
at its beauty, and then gazed about anxiously
to see if any one was coming back in search
of it.

But as no person appeared to claim it,
Hugh put it into an inside pocket, and buttoning his jacket tightly over it, said, with a
laugh: "Old Sour-Face must not see this or
he might want to walk off with it. Perhaps
some one may come to look for it to-morrow,
so I shall keep it to myself. I am sure it

belongs to that nice gentleman who gave me
the sixpence. But where is that man? If he
does not appear I shall have to run home without giving him his money."

Hugh wandered up and down for some time
longer; but not a trace of the crossing-sweeper
could he see.   At last, growing weary, he was
about to shoulder his broom and start off
home, when he caught sight of the old fellow
coming staggering towards him.

"Ha, ha, yer young warmint, yer thought
to be off with all the coin," he shouted.   "But
I 'ave yer now!   'And over what's mine, yer
young thief."

His cheeks were red, his gait unsteady, and,
seeing that the poor creature had been taking
more gin than was good for him, Hugh thought
it best to say as few words to him as possible.

"Here is your share of the money.   Thank
you for letting me sweep on your crossing," he
said, and, pushing the pennies into the man's
pocket, he ran off as fast as his stiff legs would
carry him.

The way home was long and dreary, but
Hugh heeded it not. He felt so rich and
happy that he sang out merrily as he went,

and was quite surprised when he found himself at his own door.

Poor Mrs. Brown burst into tears when she saw him enter the house, covered with mud. But Hugh only laughed; and shaking his curly head, threatened to throw his arms round her neck if she did not cheer up and look pleased.

"I earned two and ninepence to-day, mother, and I'll get more to-morrow," he cried. "So you must not be miserable because I'm not clean. No fellow could be after a day in the mud; but, all the same, I feel as happy as"—

"My own brave boy, my good little Hugh," whispered his mother, through her tears. "But come, dear, you must warm yourself and change your clothes at once. Your father is asleep; so slip into the parlor and stay there by the fire, till I get you some hot water to wash in."

"Mother, mother," cried Hugh, laughing, "are you dreaming? Just look at the state I am in. Why, if I went into the parlor, you would have to send for the mud-man to cart away the mud. But here's the money. Count it whilst I am having a scrub," and, with a joyful heart, the boy climbed up the rickety stair to the attic where he slept.

And great was the amount of scrubbing and scraping he went through before the mud was all gone; but, at last, with shining cheeks, he crept softly into the parlor and sat down on the floor at his mother's feet.

"Hoo, Hoo, 'ou a dood, dood boy," cried tiny Susie, flinging herself into his arms. "Me loves 'ou so muts, so muts, betause 'ou bring plenty pennies to muver."

"My poor boy, what a long weary day you have had, and how hard you must have worked," cried his mother, pressing him to her heart. "This money will be a help to me."

"Oh, but I shall get plenty more, mother dear. I'll go to the crossing every day till father gets well. There was an old chap there that let me sweep in his place, if I promised to give him half what I earned. Only for that I'd have had five shillings and six pence to bring home. Think of that, mother. Why, if I get that every day we'll be quite rich."

"But I do not like the work for you, Hugh. It is too like begging. I cannot bear to think of my son doing such work; I cannot, indeed. It is hard and disagreeable, and unfit for a gentleman's child."

"Yes, mother, I know it is. But still, as I

am small, there is not much that I can do.
When people are poor they must just do whatever turns up. They ought not to be proud.
I would not like to spend all my life on a crossing; and, please God, I'll soon get something
better to do."

"I hope and trust you may, dear lad, for
the very thought of. what you are at drives
me wild. I would not dare to tell your
father."

"No, mother, do not tell him. It would
vex him, I know. But still I must go on; you
must not prevent me going to-morrow, mother;
say you won't."

"My child, I cannot for we want the money
so badly. You may go to-morrow; but I shall
ask our landlady if · she knows any one who
wants an errand boy."

"Anything you like, mother. My only
wish is to help you as much as I can."

"You are a good boy, Hugh, a dear good
boy. But come, I must give you your tea.
You are very hungry, I am sure."

"I should just think I was," cried Hugh,
gayly, for his mother's words of praise had
filled his heart with joy. "I am so hungry
that I am afraid I shall eat up all that I have

earned, and you won't have gained anything after all my work on the crossing."

So Hugh was merry, and chatted and laughed as he ate his supper, never saying a word of the fatigue he felt, lest his mother should think he had really suffered, and begin to fret about his health.

"Take me to de crossing, Hoo," cried Susie, as she listened with delight to his stories of the beautiful ladies and fine carriages he saw there. "I tink it would be very nice to seep up de mud vis a broom and see all de pitty people."

But Hugh only smiled, and told her that she must grow big first, or old Sour-Face would run off with her and keep her for his own little girl.

And, at last, the poor boy grew drowsy; his merry tales became short, and he fell fast asleep before the fire.

With great difficulty his mother got him up to his room, where she put him to bed, as if he were a babe once more; and as she covered him up and kissed his happy face, she prayed that God would keep him innocent and good, amidst the dangers and temptations that were growing up around him.

CHAPTER III.

HUGH MAKES A FRIEND.

THE next morning Hugh was early at the crossing, and, as old Sour-Face was nowhere to be seen, he took his stand there at once.

But he soon found it dreary, disheartening work. A sharp wind had set in during the night, and the streets became so dry and clean that there was little sweeping to be done and no money to be earned.

So as time passed on and his pockets remained empty, Hugh grew very miserable. He was cold, tired, and hungry; but, as he had not taken a single copper, he could not buy even a crust of bread.

But as he stood, swinging his broom disconsolately to and fro in his hand, thinking sadly of the sudden failure of all his hopes, an unknown friend came to his assistance.

A good-natured "cabby," seeing the boy so wretched and cold, took him by the hand, and, leading him into the pretty shelter in Northumberland Avenue, treated him to a cup of hot coffee and a piece of bread.

Very much refreshed and full of gratitude to the stranger for his kindness, Hugh was about to return to the crossing, when he suddenly remembered the pocket-book that he had found the day before in the mud.

He had been so tired and excited after his hard work that he had forgotten to say anything about it to his mother. He now began to wonder who the owner could be.

So when the cabmen went off to their stand and he found himself alone, he drew out the book and examined it carefully.

It was very handsome, of rich, dark leather, with silver corners, and the letters "H. R." artistically entwined in a finely-wrought monogram. But there was no name, no address; and, as Hugh turned it over and over, he could find nothing that would help him to restore it to its owner.

"It is very thick and must be full of valuable papers. I do wish I knew who it belonged to," he thought. "The best way to find out all about it would be to open it and look at the things inside. But it is locked, and I do not like to burst it open until I ask mother about it. Well, there is nothing to be done on the crossing to-day, I am sure; so I think I will run off at once and ask her what she would advise me to do."

So, buttoning up the precious book in his pocket, he took up his broom and trudged away home.

When Susie saw her brother coming up the stairs, she ran to meet him with a cry of joy. But he was too full of business to trouble much about her; so putting her gently aside, he knocked at the door of his father's room.

"Mother," he whispered, "come out to me for a minute."

"Why, Hugh, what brings you home, dear?" she asked, in surprise. "Is there no work to be done to-day?"

"Not much, mother dear; but it will be better to-morrow," he answered, quickly. "Look here, I found this on the crossing. I want you to tell me what I am to do with it."

"Restore it to its owner at once, dear boy," she said. "It is very handsome, and must belong to some rich man."

"Oh, de lovely boot — de lovely boot," cried Susie; "Dive it to me, Hoo. Dive it to me, 'ou own 'ittle sissy."

"No, no, dear; I can't," he said, smiling. "I must give it back to the gentleman who lost it. But, mother dear, how shall I ever find him? I have no key to open it with, and there is no address outside. Shall I break the lock, and see if there is anything inside to tell us who the owner is?"

"Yes, I suppose you must, dear."

"It seems such a pity," said Hugh. "But, good gracious, why there it goes!"

As he spoke, the lock flew open as if by magic, and something fell out of the pocket-book, and rolled into a corner. It looked bright and pretty, so Susie dived after it; and, with dancing eyes, held up a beautiful diamond ring that flashed out radiantly in the firelight.

"Muver, muver, look what I have found," cried the child. "Oh, it is a boofle sing!"

"But, it is not yours, dear," said Hugh, gently. "The rings and this money," holding up a crisp ten-pound note, "belong to the gentleman who dropped the pocket-book, yesterday."

"But 'ou found it," said Susie, pouting, "and I want to teep it wedgy muts."

"No, no, Susie, that would not be honest; and God does not love children who are not honest and good. We must give it back as soon as we can. But, mother, wasn't it strange the way it flew open? I suppose it was some secret spring that I touched by accident."

"I suppose so, dear. But what are you to do with these treasures, Hugh? Is there no name — no address?"

"I do not see any, mother; but, perhaps, it's amongst these papers. I do wish I could find out who it belongs to."

"Teep it 'ousef, Hoo — teep it 'ousef," cried Susie, gayly, as she hopped round the room on one leg. "Janie Wheeler found sipsence and she buyed such a lot of seets."

"Little tempter," cried Hugh, laughing. "I suppose you would like me to spend this on sweets, eh?" and he waved the bank-note above his head.

"Put it away, Hugh," said his mother. "It is better not to make a joke of such a thing."

"Oh, mother dear, if it were only ours," he cried. "Think of all it would do for us."

"But it is not ours, dear boy. Do not

think of such a thing for an instant. It is a
dangerous thought, and might lead to sin. My
Hugh has surely not forgotten the Tenth Com-
mandment, that forbids us to covet anything
belonging to our neighbor?"

"No, mother, of course not," said the boy,
gently; and laying the note aside, he continued his search amongst the papers.

"Here is something," he said presently.
"It is just possible that this may be the right
address," and he handed a little packet to his
mother.

Mrs. Brown took it from him; and as she
examined it, her face flushed and her eyes
filled with tears.

"What is it, mother?" cried Hugh, throwing his arms round her neck. "Why do you
weep?"

"Look," she said, and opening the paper she
showed him what it contained : two little silken
curls, one dark, the other fair, tied together with
a faded blue ribbon ; outside the parcel were the
words : "Theo and her child, 18—; 102 Holland Park."

"It is very pretty hair, mother," said Hugh.
"But why should it make you cry?"

"Because, dear, I had once a sweet sister,

called Theo. Her hair was dark, and grew in soft curls like that. But she is dead—dead many years, now."

"Poor little mother. But I never knew you had a sister," said the boy, in surprise. "You never told me of her. I thought you and father never had any brothers and sisters."

"I had one sister, Hugh; and she was kind-hearted and loving. But I never talked to you about my family before. I displeased my father when I was young, Hugh, and he cast me off. Then I went to Australia, and never saw any of them again. When I came back to London all were dead—father, mother, and sister. Poor little Theo had married, but died soon after. So they told me at my father's old offices in the city. Their information was scant, but enough for me. Since they were dead I cared to hear no more, and so it happened that I never even heard who my sister married."

"No," said Hugh, thoughtfully. "Well, do you know, mother, I think that was a pity, for he might have been a friend to us had you found him out. He might have helped us for the sake of his dead wife."

"So he might, dearest, and I shall make

inquiries. It is just possible that he might help you to something to earn your bread, poor boy."

"Yes, wouldn't that be splendid? Why, mother, I wonder you did not think of this long ago."

"I did, dearest. But it seemed so hopeless," said Mrs. Brown, with a sigh, as folding up the little packet she replaced it in the pocketbook. "And now, dear boy, let us consider what it is best to do with this."

"I shall take it off at once to Holland Park," said Hugh, decidedly. "It's contents are very valuable, and I shall be glad to get rid of it."

"But you are tired, to-day, Hugh. Don't you think you might wait till the morning?"

"No, mother; I think it would be better to go at once. I am not at all tired, I assure you. I am longing to give that poor gentleman his precious book. I am sure he is in a terrible way about it."

"Well, perhaps, it would be best to return it at once; but, Hugh, put on another suit and make yourself neat."

"Of course, mother dear," said Hugh, gaily. "You don't imagine that I'm going to introduce myself as a crossing-sweeper at Holland Park!"

" I most sincerely hope not," said his mother, gravely. "It would not be necessary to mention the fact of your ever having done such degrading work."

"Trust me, mother mine. I shall not forget that my father is a gentleman, and that my mother is—well, fit to be a countess," and giving her a loving kiss, he ran off to perform his toilet.

And when the boy came down, about half an hour later, dressed and ready for his walk, his mother was well satisfied with his appearance; she felt that no one could take him for anything but a little gentleman.

Then she insisted on giving him his dinner, before he started; and so, though Hugh hurried as much as possible, it was nearly six o'clock before he left the house.

It is a long way from Tavistock Square to Holland Park; and as Hugh had walked many miles that day, it would not have been astonishing had he felt a little tired. But he was so full of delight at the thoughts of the pleasure he was about to give the owner of the pocketbook, that he did not feel the slightest fatigue as he pushed his way through the crowded streets.

The shops looked very tempting in the brilliant gas-light, and he stopped now and again to gaze at the flaxen-haired dolls that hung in the windows.

"Some day when I am rich, as rich as the Lord Mayor, or maybe sooner, I'll buy one of those for Susie. Won't she be proud and pleased, poor little soul," he said. "But, I really must shut my eyes to these pretty things, or I shan't reach Holland Park to-night." And then he ran on whistling and singing, determined not to look at another shop till he was on his way home again.

But when, at last he reached his destination, a great fear came over him. The house looked so large and splendid, that poor Hugh felt inclined to drop the pocket-book into the letter-box and run away.

"But that would be cowardly," he said to himself, "and the right gentleman might never get his beautiful things; for perhaps he does not live here at all."

So, plucking up all the courage he could muster, he walked slowly up to the hall-door steps and rang the bell.

But no notice was taken of his gentle summons; so, having waited patiently for several minutes, he rang again. This time he was more successful, and he heard the bell peal loudly through the lower part of the house.

Footsteps were soon heard approaching, and before Hugh had time to think of what he should say, the massive door swung back on its hinges, and a gorgeous being in plush and powder stood in the doorway.

"Now, then, an' wat do you want?" he asked, indignantly. "Small boys like you have no business to ring the bell so loud."

"I want to see the gentleman of this house, very particularly," said Hugh, drawing himself up proudly, and speaking with much dignity. "Will you please to tell him so?"

"I'll please to tell him nothink of the sort, young gentleman. Give me your message and I'll deliver it. My master never sees nobody at night. He's at his dessert, an' must not be disturbed."

"Oh, but please, I'm sure he will see me," said Hugh, earnestly. "I have come a long way and— But please give him this packet and see what he will say."

The man took the paper in which were wrapped the silken curls, looked at the inscription, and, with a softened expression and manner, asked Hugh to walk in and sit down.

Hugh entered the hall, and stood upon the mat, wondering nervously what would happen next, as he saw the servant disappear, carrying the little packet on a salver.

But he was not kept long in suspense. In a few seconds a door was quickly opened, and a tall, gentlemanly looking man came forward and laid his hand upon his shoulder.

"You are a welcome sight, my little man," he said, " for by this packet, I know you must have found my pocket-book."

" Yes, sir," said Hugh, drawing forth the book, and handing it to him. " I found it on the crossing at the end of the Strand, near Trafalgar Square, yesterday. It is just as I found it, except that I took out the packet. It was upon it I saw the address."

" Yes," said the gentleman. " But are you not afraid to give it to me? Are you quite certain it belongs to me?"

" Oh, yes, sir; I am sure — I feel certain."

" Very well. But just to prove that it is mine really, and lest you should have any misgivings in the future, I will tell you a few things that are in it. There is a diamond ring, with one stone missing, with the words ' till death' engraved inside, and "—

" Oh, yes; but, please, I know it is yours," cried Hugh. "So please take—please take it."

" Very well, my boy, since you are satisfied, so am I. Allow me to thank you most sincerely," said the gentleman, and he shook Hugh warmly by the hand. " And now, what is your name? Mine is Sir Henry Randall."

" Hugh Brown, Sir Henry."

" A good, honest name. Well, now, Master Hugh, come in and take a glass of wine with me."

" Please, I don't drink wine," said Hugh, " I "—

" And quite right, too. Little lads, like you, do not require it. But come in and have a few minutes' talk with me. I want to go over the contents of my pocket-book, just to see that none of the papers have dropped out. I shall feel great pleasure in giving you the reward."

" But I do not want a reward," said Hugh. " I brought you back your pocket-book, as soon as I knew the address, Sir Henry; but I never thought of a reward."

" Indeed," said Sir Henry, smiling. " But,

come in, and tell me something about yourself. You have done me a great service, and I cannot allow you to run away in such a hurry."

So, Hugh was obliged to follow the master of the house, and soon found himself seated before a table covered with dainties, the like of which he had never seen in his life before.

And, at a sign from Sir Henry, the magnificent being in plush and powder supplied him with fruit and cake, waiting upon him as gravely and politely as if he were the Prince of Wales himself. At least, so thought simple Hugh.

And as the boy was eating the delicacies with which he had been provided, Sir Henry stood at the mantle-piece in silence. He emptied the pocket-book and examined carefully all the papers it contained.

" You can go, Thomas," he said, turning round suddenly. And when the man had disappeared, he went forward, and laid his hand upon Hugh's curly head.

" You are a good, honest lad," he said; " and I shall never be able to repay you for what you have done for me. There are things in this book that no money could ever replace. I did not remember about this note when I offered the reward, or I should have been obliged to offer more. Had a dishonest person found it, I might never have seen it again. Fortunately for me, it fell into your hands, and so I have received it just as it was when I lost it."

"But, please, I only did my duty, Sir Henry," said Hugh, blushing.

"Yes, of course; but here is your reward, my boy. I would advise you to buy something useful with it." And to Hugh's surprise the crisp bank-note that he had shown to Susy was laid before him.

"Please, Sir Henry, I do not want it. I would rather not take it," said Hugh, shrinking away from the note.

"But, my dear lad, it is your own," said Sir Henry, kindly. "And no one need be ashamed to take what is his own. There are few boys so rich, that they would not be glad to have a little more money. Come, now, aren't there a great many things, you would like to buy?"

"Oh, yes," stammered Hugh, "but —"

"But what?"

"I don't think mother would like me to take the money," he answered, blushing violently. "And so, please, I would rather not."

" Well, is there anything I can get for you, Hugh? Anything you would like as a present? For I must do something, to show that I am not ungrateful for the service you have done me. Speak, child, what can I do for you?"

" There is one thing, Sir Henry," said Hugh, boldly. " I want to get some work to do, to earn money and help my mother. If you could help me to get that, I would be truly thankful."

" My poor lad; but you are very small and young to think of working. Wait till you are a little older."

" But I can't wait," cried Hugh. " Father is ill, and we want money so badly. Poor mother frets so much about it. And, oh, I would so love to help her."

" And so you shall, dear lad," said Sir Henry, with emotion. " I have a large business in the city, and want many boys in my office. If you do not think that beneath you, I am sure I shall be able to find you a place there. Leave me your address and I will go and see your mother about it."

" Oh, sir, sir, you are very good," cried Hugh, his eyes dancing with joy, as he wrote his address upon a piece of paper, and handed it to Sir Henry. "I will work so hard — so hard."

"Yes, you must be sure to do that, little man," said Sir Henry, smiling. "That is the real way to get on. The pay will not be large at first; but, if you are clever and industrious, you may sometime or other find yourself in a good position. But, now, do not be proud. Take your ten pounds; they will help your mother to get many things she must want for your sick father."

"Yes, so they would. But — but "—

"Come, now, you must take them," said Sir Henry; and folding the note he slipped it into the boy's pocket. "And now I want to introduce you to my children. They will be pleased to see you, when I tell them you have brought back my precious pocket-book."

Then, taking Hugh by the hand, he led him out of the dining-room, and down a large, well-lighted hall.

And the whole place seemed so beautiful to the simple boy, that he began to think he had found his way suddenly into fairyland.

CHAPTER IV.

PERCY AT HOME.

"HA! Percy is in a good humor, I perceive. Well, so much the better," said Sir Henry to himself, as, opening a side door, he walked down the gayly-decorated passage, that led to his son's apartment.

"These are my boy's flowers, Hugh," he remarked. "Flowers and music are the delight of his life. Hark! do you hear that music? Well, that is my son. We always know what his thoughts are, by the way he plays. If he is gay, his music is gay; if he is sad, he brings forth the most melancholy sounds possible. To-night, he seems to be in a most amiable mood; so we are lucky."

As Sir Henry spoke, the solemn tones of an organ came swelling through the air, and Hugh listened with delight to the harmonious sounds.

"You are fond of music, my little man," said his new friend. "I am glad of that. I think it a good sign in any one. But come in softly. We must not disturb Percy whilst he plays."

Then, raising a crimson curtain that hung in the doorway, Sir Henry drew Hugh into a large, handsomely furnished room.

Here our little friend stood spell-bound in astonishment, touched to the heart by what he saw.

At one end of the room was a magnificent organ, and upon the high stool before it, sat a quaint-looking boy of about eleven years old. His face was pale and fair, with the delicate complexion of a girl, whilst long, golden curls fell in rich profusion over his velvet coat, veiling, but, alas! not concealing what was only too visible, that the poor boy was completely deformed. Hugh felt the tears rise quickly to his eyes, as he gazed at the humped back, and thought how sad it must be to be made in such a manner, unable to run or jump as other boys did. And in his heart he thanked God for having made him straight and strong.

"Oh, papa dear, I am so glad that you have come in at last," cried a sweet voice; and a pretty, dark-eyed girl ran forward to greet Sir Henry.

"Hush, Theo. Wait till Percy has done playing. You know we must not disturb him, my child," whispered her father, laying his hand caressingly upon her head.

"I wish he would stop playing, then," she cried, peevishly. "I'm quite tired of his organ."

"Theo," exclaimed her father; and he looked so stern, that the little girl shook herself away from him, and seated herself at the table. Meanwhile, the boy at the organ seemed unconscious of their presence, so absorbed was he in his music.

And as Hugh stood listening in silence he looked around the room with mingled feelings of wonder and delight. Never before had he seen so many beautiful things — things that all boys love and admire.

There were books in rich bindings; fishing-rods, bats and balls, a gun, and a small pistol; at the furthest end of the room stood a full-rigged yacht and a splendid telescope; over the mantlepiece was a wonderful arrangement of swords of every shape and size, and the walls were hung with pictures of famous horses and dogs.

"How happy these children must be in such a beautiful room," he thought. "What a lucky boy he is to have—and yet"— And he sighed, as his eyes rested once more upon the poor little figure at the organ.

At last a loud, prolonged chord sounded through the room, and the musician turned round upon his seat. The peaceful look that he had worn whilst playing had disappeared, and an expression of discontent now marred the beauty of his face.

But when he saw his father, he smiled brightly, and slipped down quickly from his perch on the music-stool.

"So you have come, at last, father?" he said. "Theo was growing impatient. She says the tea is quite spoiled."

"I could not come any sooner," said his father, kissing him tenderly. "I had business to attend to after dinner. But see, I have brought you a visitor."

"Who is he?" whispered Percy, flushing, and darting a look of keen inquiry at Hugh, who stood shyly in the doorway. "I never saw him before."

"No; he is a new friend of mine, Percy. You and Theo must treat him very well. He is a fine fellow, and has just done me a great service.   Come, Hugh, come over here and shake hands with these young people.   That's right.   And now, Theo dear, let us have some tea, and I shall tell you what this good boy has done for me."

"What was it, papa?" cried Theo.   "Do tell us.   I am just dying to hear something besides that organ.   My ears are ringing with it."

"It's better than your perpetual chatter, any way," muttered Percy, with an angry look at his sister.

"Oh, that doesn't trouble you much," replied Theo.   "You never listen to it."

"Not when I can help it certainly.   But do stop, Theo, and let us hear what papa has to tell us," cried Percy.   "You are a dreadful chatterbox."

"Hush, children, do not quarrel, please," said their father.   "Take some cake, Hugh. Well, Percy, I was going to tell you what this little man has done for me.   But you don't seem inclined to listen.

"Yes, yes, father," cried Percy.   "But Theo will keep teasing me."

"Now, Percy, you know I did not begin. It was all your fault."

But, as Sir Henry took no notice of this remark, the children subsided quietly. Percy helped himself to cake, and turned his back on his sister; whilst she applied herself to pouring out the tea.

" The other day, Percy," began Sir Henry, " I told you, I think, that I had lost a pocket-book, containing some valuable letters, and " —

" Yes, and poor mamma's hair," cried Percy, now completely interested in the story.

" Yes; my boy. Your dear mother's hair, that I would not have lost for all the world. And besides this, Percy, there was her ring that wanted a little repairing; a ten-pound note which I had quite forgotten about, and several other things, more or less valuable. Had a rogue found the book I should have lost everything. I only offered ten pounds' reward, and that would never have tempted a thief to give up so much."

" And did this little fellow find the book and bring it back to you? " asked Percy, the bright look coming into his face again.

" Yes, Percy; he brought it back whole and intact. Never dreaming of touching a penny of the money, at a time when a few pounds would be of great value to those he loves dearly."

"Well, I am glad to see you," cried Percy, shaking the boy once more by the hand. "But when did you find the pocket-book? And how did you know it was papa's?"

"One question at a time, Percy lad," said his father, laughing. "Now, Hugh, tell us all about it please. How did you come to find the pocket-book?"

"I was standing at the crossing in Trafalgar Square, Sir Henry, when you went past," said Hugh, flushing, and longing to tell his new friends what he had been doing there. They all looked so kind that he felt sure they would not be at all shocked, if he told them why he had taken to such work. But he remembered his mother's injunctions, and said nothing about it. "You threw a bright sixpence to a little crossing-sweeper and hurried on."

"Did I really? Why, you must have uncommonly sharp eyes, Master Hugh," said Sir Henry, looking up with a laugh.

"I have — rather," said Hugh, laughing and blushing. "Well, a minute after that, I saw something lying in the mud. I picked it up and rubbed it clean. It was the pocket-book."

"It was a good thing the crossing-sweeper didn't find it," cried Percy, "for it's very likely he would have kept it. They are terrible little ragamuffins, I believe."

"Not always," said Hugh, with a twinkle in his eye. "However, I put the book in my pocket and went home. There it lay till the next morning, and then I spent hours trying to open it, to find if there was any address inside. But I could not manage it, and was about to break the lock when, all at once, it flew open in my hands."

"Well, that was funny," said Theo. "I remember when papa bought that book, Percy and I worked at it for ever so long, and it never opened."

"I suppose I touched some spring by accident," said Hugh. "I had worked at it for a good while, too, and had almost given up in despair, when it suddenly opened, and the beautiful ring rolled away into a corner."

"But I hope you found it again?" cried Theo, quickly.

"Oh, yes; in a minute. Susie crept after it and wanted to keep it," said Hugh, laughing. "But I soon got it back from her."

"But it was wicked to want to keep it, when

it wasn't hers," remarked Theo, severely. "Susie can't be a very honest person, I am afraid."

"But she is only four years old," cried Hugh. "The poor mite did not mean any harm."

"Is Susie your little sister, Hugh?" asked Sir Henry, smiling.

"Yes, sir; my only sister. And she's such a darling."

"I am sorry I said she wasn't honest, Hugh," whispered Theo. "But she shall have something far nicer than a ring. I am sure she would like a big wax doll. Wouldn't she now?"

"I am sure she would, Miss Theo," answered Hugh, brightly. "She has only an old piece of wood, that I dressed up as a doll for her. She would go wild at the sight of a real wax one, I know."

"Then she shall have a beauty. I am too old for dolls, now, and I have such a pretty one upstairs. Papa, do you know, Aunt Ethel thinks I'm a baby still, and keeps sending me dolls every birthday. Isn't it too bad?"

"Well, you can hardly expect Aunt Ethel to know what a wise person you are, Theo," said her father, taking her on his knee, and stroking her long hair. "Most girls of ten like dolls. But do you know, Hugh, this young lady cares only for books, and hates dolls, toys, and, above all, music."

"No, no, papa," cried Theo, glancing quickly at her brother. "I love music, but Percy keeps on dinning."

"Well, never mind Percy, but run off and get this wonderful doll for Susie," cried Sir Henry, quickly. "It is getting late, and Hugh has a long way to go. Haven't you, my boy?"

"Yes, Sir Henry; to John Street, Tavistock Square," said Hugh. "I think I must soon be off, as my mother will be anxious."

"So she will," said Sir Henry. "So be quick and get the doll, Theo."

"Yes, papa; I shall not be a minute," she answered, gayly. And away she went out of the room, and up the broad staircase, to her own little chamber where she kept her treasures.

"I am glad there is a doll for Miss Susie," said Sir Henry. "It will make up to her for the loss of the ring; eh, Percy?"

But Percy did not respond; he flushed

slightly — moved uneasily on his chair, and began to crumble his cake upon his plate.

Very soon they heard Theo running down the passage, and in a moment she burst into the room again. Her cheeks were flushed, her eyes flashing with anger, and darting up to Percy she stamped her foot, exclaiming: "You naughty boy! How dare you go to my toy cupboard? How dare you touch my things and break " — But words failed her and she sobbed aloud.

Percy frowned, and a sulky look came into his eyes.

"It was no use to you, Theo. You have plenty of other dolls that you never touch. I wanted to see what made that one speak," he grumbled. "I wish you wouldn't make such a fuss about nothing."

"Fuss about nothing — is that what you call nothing?" she sobbed out. "I wanted to give that baby doll to Susie, and there I find it all broken and destroyed. But, Kapes says, hunchbacks are always mischievous, and " —

At these words Percy sprang to his feet, crimson with passion. He glared for an instant at his sister, and seizing a plate hurled it wildly at her head. Then turning deadly pale, uttered a cry of horror, and fell back in his chair, trembling violently.

Fortunately, the girl saw the dangerous missile leave the boy's hand, and as she stepped quickly aside, the plate went flying past her, and was smashed to atoms against the wall. Horrified at this outburst, she gazed at her brother in surprise. Then, remembering that it was her fault; that her words had angered him, she flung herself on her knees by his side.

"Percy, dear, I am so sorry; I will never say such a thing again," she cried. "I did not mean to vex you, indeed, I did not."

But Percy turned away, and deep groans escaped his quivering lips.

"Theo," said Sir Henry, sternly, "you are a most unfeeling girl. How could you say such unkind things? Go to your room immediately."

Theo rose up, sobbing bitterly, and was about to hurry away, when Percy put out his hand and drew her towards him.

"My sister, my dear little sister," he cried, kissing her passionately. "I am very wicked — very wicked — but, oh, you must forgive me. Papa, you must forgive me, too — you must forgive us both, for we have no

mother!" and burying his face in his hand,
Percy burst into tears.

"My poor boy, my poor little man," cried
his father, laying his hand upon the bowed
head. "But do not take things so much to
heart. I am sorry that Theo and you should
be so violent. You must try to be more kind
and gentle to each other; but do not fret. I
forgive you, of course. See, you have frightened Hugh with your extraordinary behavior.
But come, my boy, cheer up. Hugh, I think
you had better say, good-night. You have a
long way to go and it is getting late."

Hugh dried up the tears that had begun
to flow at the sight of Percy's unhappiness;
shook hands with the boy nervously, and taking
up his hat went quickly out of the room. He
looked about for Theo to wish her good-night,
but she had disappeared, and so he hurried
after Sir Henry.

"There is a cab at the door, Hugh," said his
kind friend, "and I wish you to go home in it.
It is too late for you to walk through the
streets alone. I shall not forget my promise
of work; but will see about it at once. I shall
go down some day, soon, and talk over matters with your mother."

" Oh, thank you, Sir Henry."

" I am only afraid that I shall not be able to do much for you, as you are so small," said Sir Henry, thoughtfully. " A boy of twelve cannot do much. Would you be content to run messages ? "

"Yes; indeed, I would. I would do anything at which I could earn a few shillings a week, and so help mother a little, till my father gets well again."

"And that you shall certainly do before long. But, remember, Hugh, if I once give you a start, the rest will depend upon yourself. If you work hard, you may rise in time, for you are a clever boy, I am sure. If you care to work, you may be a rich man some day."

Overcome with gratitude at so much kindness and encouragement, Hugh was speechless. He could not find words to express his feelings, so seizing Sir Henry's hand, he covered it with kisses, and darted out of the house.

Just as he was about to step into the cab, a little figure with streaming ribbons, and tear-stained face came flying down the hall. It was Theo, and in her hand she carried a parcel.

" Hugh, Hugh," she called, running out

upon the door-step, "take this and give it to little Susie. It is a doll—not a big one, or half so pretty as the one Percy broke, but still she will like it, I hope."

"Oh, Miss Theo, you are too good," cried Hugh, as he took the parcel from her hand. "You are so kind, so "—

Then he turned and ran down the steps, as fast as he could. He felt the tears rushing back into his eyes, and he could say no more.

It was very late when Hugh reached home; and as he ran up stairs, his mother met him with anxious looks and eager inquiries.

She listened joyfully to his happy tale, and thanked God from her heart, for the good fortune that had come to her boy.

"And did you not feel jealous of all the beautiful things you saw around those children, Hugh, darling?"

"Not a bit, mother dear," he answered, as he flung his arms around her. "They are rich —but not as rich as I am; for the poor things have no mother."

CHAPTER V.

SUSIE HAS A TREAT.

THE next morning Susie tripped into the sitting room, with joyous steps and smiling face.

Whilst dressing her, her mother had told her that Hugh would take her for a walk, as he was not going to work on the crossing any more. This was good news for Susie, for the greatest treat she could imagine, was to toddle off through the streets with her big brother.

Everything was ready for breakfast, the room all nice and tidy, and Susie looked round, expecting to see Hugh seated comfortably by the fire, in his father's arm-chair.

He was nowhere to be seen, however; but oh, joy! in his place was a lovely doll, with a pretty blue frock and a mop of golden curls.

The little girl gave a cry of delight, and

darting forward, caught the beautiful creature in her arms.

"Ha, ha," laughed Hugh, running out from the back of the chair; "ha, ha, Miss Susican, that's something like a dolly, I think!"

"Oh, Hoo, Hoo," she cried, kissing him rapturously. "See is a booty — see is a booty. Did 'ou find her in the mud, too?"

"In the mud, Susie, I should rather think not," and Hugh laughed so loudly at such an idea, that he brought his mother in to see what was going on.

"Do not make so much noise, dear boy," she said; "it disturbs poor father."

"Oh, mudder, mudder," cried Susie, with eager delight, "look at the dolly Hoo binged me. Isn't see lubly? Isn't see a booty?"

"She is a beauty indeed, darling, and you must take great care of her. But, Hugh, I want you both to be very quiet to-day. What would you say to taking Susie to see the Lord Mayor's show? They say it will be very fine."

"But we should have to go so far away, mother, and you might want me."

"No, no, dear, I shan't want you at all. Your father is much better, and seems inclined to sleep; so the best thing for him is to keep the place as quiet as possible."

" Very well, mother; but still " —

" No buts, dear," said his mother, smiling. " I want you to have a happy day, Hugh. You have been so good and worked so hard, that you deserve a treat. So off you go for a fine long run."

" Well, I should like one, mammy, and I dare say Susie will enjoy it too," he said, gayly. " Give us some bread and butter in our pockets, and we'll set off as soon as breakfast is over."

" Oh, joy, joy," shouted Susie; " and Dolly sall go too — see sall — see sall."

But both her mother and Hugh objected to this, as Dolly might get spoiled as they pushed their way through the crowd.

Susie was in despair at the thoughts of not taking her darling; and it was some time before they could persuade her to go out and leave her.

" I'll buy you a cake, Susie," said Hugh, coaxingly; " and, who knows, perhaps we might come home in an omnibus. Wouldn't that be nice, little woman?"

" Hoo, Hoo, dat would be nice," cried the

child; and the doll was put to bed in a corner, and away trotted Susie to get ready for her walk.

And at last the two children started off, Susie radiantly happy as she went along, her hand in Hugh's.

But it was not altogether pleasant walking through the streets, as they were very muddy and slippery.

"I think I must carry you, dear, or you'll be covered with mud," said her careful brother.

But just at this moment, his friend, "the cabby," appeared, and taking them up on the box beside him, drove them off to Trafalgar Square.

This was a capital place for seeing the show on its way to Westminster, and the little people were in high glee as they stood waiting for the great procession.

They had taken their stand in front of the National Bank, and Hugh promised to lift Susie on his shoulder, whenever he heard the band approaching.

The windows of the Bank above were filled with gayly dressed people, and Hugh began to wish that he and Susie were there, away from the mud and the crowd. Looking up suddenly, he was surprised to see a pretty, dark-eyed girl smiling and bowing to him; in a few minutes the heavy window was raised a little, and Theo Randall called out to him to go up to her at once.

But this was not an easy matter. When Hugh presented himself at the door, and asked leave to go up to the young lady, the porter laughed at him, and asked him for his ticket. The boy was obliged to confess that he had none, but that a friend had beckoned to him, and told him to go up to her.

"A very likely story, young 'un. But I'm not so green as to be caught that way. Just you sheer off with yourself," said the man, and Hugh turned away without a word.

"Hugh, Hugh, come back," called a small voice, imperiously; and looking up he saw Theo standing at the top of the steps.

"He is my friend, and we have plenty of room up stairs," she said, grandly; and the man bowed and held the door open as Hugh and Susie entered the hall.

"I am glad to see you again," said Theo. "And is this Susie? What a dear little mite she is. But come, Percy will be angry if we stand here talking too long. Now, Susie, take my hand, and I'll help you up the stairs." But the child held back nervously. She felt shy and frightened at the sight of this smart young lady in her velvet and fur.

"She's very shy, Miss Randall," said Hugh, "for she's not accustomed to strangers."

"Oh, I've got a cure for shyness," said Theo, and drawing a packet of chocolate creams from her muff, she began to pop them into Susie's mouth.

"Aren't they good, dear?" she asked, with a smile.

"Wery dood," answered Susie; and her small heart was conquered at once.

When the three children entered the room above, Percy was sitting at the window, looking very cross.

"What a time you have been, Theo," he cried, peevishly; "one would think it was a mile to the door."

"Well, I couldn't help it, dear," answered his sister, soothingly. "The porter would not allow Hugh to come up to us; but I made him, and here he is. Come over here, Hugh."

"That's right, Theo," replied Percy, becoming quite amiable, and holding out his hand to Hugh. "I am very glad to see you again. I hope your father is better?"

"Yes, thank you; he is a good deal better to-day."

"I am very glad to hear it. Is that your little sister?"

"Yes. Come, Susie, and shake hands with this young gentleman."

Susie went over slowly, gazing with wonder at Percy's golden curls and fair delicate face.

The boy's expression had changed wonderfully, since the others had entered the room. The cross look had disappeared, and his countenance was lighted up with a beautiful smile, as he turned to speak to the little girl. This, combined with his velvet suit, deep lace collar, and long, fair hair, gave him a quaint, uncommon appearance that impressed Susie greatly.

"Is him a boy, Hoo?" she whispered. "I tink him's like a wax-work."

"Oh, Susie," cried Hugh, covered with confusion.

But Percy was highly amused, and taking the child on his knee, began to question her about the wax-works, and when she had seen them.

"But is 'ou a boy?" she repeated, "a weal dood boy like my Hoo?"

"No, not a good boy, I'm afraid, Susie," he answered, quickly. "Only a bad-tempered boy, as Hugh can tell you."

The bright smile died away on his lips, and, sighing heavily, he looked out into the street.

"Come with me, little Susie," said Theo, and she drew her off with her to the other window.

But Hugh remained with Percy, hoping to cheer him up, and bring the happy smile back to the pale face once more. He talked a great deal, told funny stories, and did all he could to make his friend look bright; but his efforts were in vain.

Percy paid not the smallest attention, and did not appear to hear what he was saying; he was quite absorbed in his own gloomy thoughts.

"Hugh," he said, suddenly, "were you not very much shocked last night at my dreadful temper?"

"I was startled, Master Percy, and — a little frightened; for you might have killed Miss Theo with that plate," said Hugh, blushing.

"Yes, yes, I know. But I can't help it.
When I get into a passion — like that — I don't
know what I am doing. And oh, Hugh," he
whispered, "it is so dreadful to be a hunchback. I never can think why I was born, or
why I am allowed to live."

"Oh, Master Percy," cried Hugh, horrified
at the boy's words. "What would your father
do without you? He loves you so dearly."

"Yes, yes; he loves me and pities me. But
of what use am I to him as a son, I, a poor,
miserable hunchback?"

"But why should that make any difference?"
cried Hugh, quickly. "He does not want you
to work, and if you are good and clever"—

"Yes; if I were good and clever," said
Percy, bitterly. "But I am not—and every-
one hates me. The servants, my aunts, uncles,
and cousins—all pity papa for having such a
son; they say hunchbacks are always wicked,
and that makes me so unhappy." And leaning
his head against the window, the poor boy
burst into tears.

"They are wicked to say such a cruel thing,"
cried Hugh, indignantly. "God made you a
hunchback, Master Percy, but He loves you
just as much as if you were straight."

"Do you think so, Hugh? Do you really think so?"

"Of course I do—I know it," answered Hugh, firmly. "And as for being wicked, it all depends on ourselves. If we pray to our Heavenly Father, He will always help us to be good."

"Yes, but it is hard—and then when people don't like me, and say unkind things, it makes me angry and ill-tempered."

"But I am sure you could make people love you if you tried, Master Percy," said Hugh, gently. "I don't want to say anything to vex you; but I think if you would be kind and gentle to your friends, they would get to love you. Mother says"—

"Ah, you are a lucky boy to have your mother to talk to you. When mamma was alive it was quite different. She used to help me to be good. She talked to me of God—and, hunchback though I was—still I was her darling—her own little son. But, oh, Hugh, she died when I was six—and I shall never see her again."

"Oh, yes, Master Percy, you will surely see her in heaven."

"In heaven—alas! no; for I am too wicked to go there."

"No, no," said Hugh, earnestly. "You must not say that. God is all mercy and forgiveness, and if you try to be good, He will be sure to help you."

"But I can never remember that when I feel wicked. No one talks to me of God now. Papa is too busy. Theo knows nothing about such things, and—and I never go to church."

"Never go to church. Oh, that is very wrong. But why do you not go, Master Percy?"

"Because," said Percy, flushing painfully, "people stare at me, and I hear them whispering, 'Poor boy: what a pity,' and I can't bear it. So I just stay at home with my organ. That is the one thing that comforts me."

"But your mother would have liked you to go to church, I'm sure," said Hugh, gravely. "Don't you think so?"

"Yes, I know she would. She used always to take me. I did not mind anything when she was there. But it's very different now."

"Well, Master Percy, I'd advise you to go to church. You don't know what a comfort it is when you are in trouble. And then," said

Hugh, with a bright look, " if any one pities you, just offer the pain you feel up to God— offer it to Jesus Christ, and think of His sufferings. Once, when I was ill, mother told me to do that, and, do you know, I did not mind the pain half so much."

"You are a good boy, Hugh," cried Percy, gazing with admiration at the lad's earnest face. "If you will talk to me sometimes and help me to be good, I am sure I shall soon grow much better."

"But you must ask God to help you, Percy, and do your best to be good. Here are two lines of a hymn that will teach you to remember how ready God is to do what we ask Him :

> " Whatsoever ye ask in My Name I will do it,
>   Abide in My love, and be joyful in Me."

"I never heard those lines before," said Percy, " but I will say them over and over to myself."

"That is right," said Hugh, smiling, " and now let us be joyful, as God tells us to be."

"Percy—Hugh. Here comes the music— the band—listen—look !" cried Theo, dancing up to their window. "See ! the procession will soon begin to pass," and back she went to Susie.

But this interruption put an end to the boys' serious talk; and the sound of the dashing music helped to cheer them, and soon blew away the clouds from their brows.

"There's papa—there's papa," cried Theo, as a handsome carriage passed under the window, and Sir Henry Randall was seen bowing and smiling to his children.

"My father was once Lord Mayor," said Percy. "It was when I was a very little boy, and every one said mamma was the most beautiful Lady Mayoress they had ever seen."

"That must have been amusing," said Hugh, gayly.

"Yes, mamma liked it, and Theo had a good deal of fun, although she was only a tiny thing. But I did not like it at all," said Percy, sadly. "It was then papa was made Sir Henry; grandpapa was very proud; but mamma liked Mr. Randall best."

"Did she? Well, I think Sir Henry sounds beautiful. But what is that noise, Percy? It seems as if we were in the Zoölogical Gardens instead of in the Strand."

"Oh, I know what it is. Papa told us all about it," said Percy, laughing. "The Prince of Wales brought a number of animals from

India, and they are to make part of the show to-day."

Here shouts of delight were heard from Theo and Susie; and the two boys went over to their window, so that they might all enjoy the sight together.

The stream of carriages passed quickly along, and then a couple of gayly-caparisoned dromedaries trotted down the Strand, ridden by black-faced men in gorgeous garments.

Susie clapped her hands with delight, but when two huge elephants went roaring past, she screamed with fright, and buried her face in Hugh's sleeve.

"You poor little goosie," cried Theo, laughing. "How could they possibly touch you? But see here, Susie, look at this funny thing. It is called Cleopatra's Needle."

"A needle?" cried Susie, looking up once more. "Oh, she must be a big woman to use a needle like that—and it don't look a bit sharp."

"But it isn't a needle to use, dear," explained Theo. "It's only made to imitate a big monument or obelisk that has been brought to London, and is going to be put up somewhere—I don't know where. It is made of stone, Susie, and is covered with figures and hieroglyphics. This is only a paper affair."

"Well, it's very silly to call it a needle, for it isn't a bit like one," said Susie.

The children laughed heartily at this wise remark, and even Percy joined in the merriment as the model of the famous obelisk passed under the window, its paper sides fluttering and flapping in the wind.

Then came some camels, and finally a magnificent car, with gayly dressed figures carrying banners and flags.

"That gorgeous thing represents History, Peace and Plenty," said Percy, "and I must say it is very well done."

"Very well, indeed," said Theo. "I never saw such a good Lord Mayor's show. Those animals made it quite amusing."

"But—but I never saw a Lord Mayor at all," cried Susie. "Was he on a big elephant?"

"You funny child," said Theo, laughing. "He was in the grand carriage with some of his friends.

"Was he?" said Susie, in a disappointed voice. "Then he was just like all the other gempleman."

"Well, yes, he had only one head," said Theo, and "—

"Theo, dear," remarked Percy, "as papa is going to the banquet, I think we will have dinner in my room. I want Hugh and Susie to come home with us."

"That would be nice," cried Theo, clapping her hands. "Come along quick. The carriage is at the door."

"But we cannot go with you, Miss Theo," said Hugh. "We cannot, indeed."

"Not come? But why not?"

"Because my mother would be uneasy about us. She would "—

"We can soon put that right," cried Percy. "Come along, my boy. We will drive to Mrs. Brown's and ask her permission."

So, into the comfortable landau the children were obliged to get; and with the air of a young lady accustomed to command, Theo ordered the footman to go to 16 John's Street, Tavistock Square.

Susie was speechless with delight. Never before had she sat in a carriage; and she was afraid to breathe, lest she should wake up and find it all a dream.

When the handsome equipage entered the

narrow street where the Browns lived, many were the looks of astonishment cast upon it by young and old.

Children shouted and cheered, as they recognized their friends, Hugh and Susie; and the old people smiled at the grave dignity of the tiny maiden; and nodded pleasantly to the lad, who was a favorite with all.

Hugh sprang up the stairs to the little parlor, and flinging his arms round his mother's neck, told her of the invitation he had received.

"It will be very nice, dear," said Mrs. Brown, and scarcely realizing what she was doing, she granted the desired permission.

"Thank you, mother — thank you," cried Hugh; and away he went.

So, before Mrs. Brown had time to recover from her astonishment, or understand thoroughly what was going on, the carriage had left her door and was far away on its journey westwards.

CHAPTER VI.

THE children spent a pleasant evening in Percy's pretty room.

Theo was enchanted with Susie, and did all she could to amuse her. And she was so completely absorbed in her new plaything, that she did not quarrel once with her brother.

The boys had many tastes in common, and Percy had never felt so happy in the company of any child before. Hugh was good tempered, bright, and brave, and his very presence seemed to calm the nervous, irritable Percy.

" How I wish you were my brother, or even my cousin, Hugh," said Percy. " Wouldn't it be jolly if you were my cousin?"

" Yes," said Hugh, laughing, " I daresay it would. But as I never had a cousin, I can't exactly say."

" Oh, I have plenty of them — but they're

all such queer chaps. I find it very hard to get on with any of them. Now, if you were my cousin, I'd like to have you always with me."

"That would be very kind of you," answered Hugh. "But supposing I wouldn't stay?"

"Oh, I'd chain you up, and make you. But come along and play me a game of Bezique."

So the time passed very happily; and it was a real sorrow for the young Randalls when, early next morning, Hugh and Susie took their departure.

They did all they could to make them stay till the afternoon, at least. But Hugh was determined to go home. He was anxious to know how his father was, and nothing that his friends could do, or say, would make him change his mind.

Susie was very angry with her brother, and wept bitterly. She implored him to stay till after luncheon, and then go home in the carriage. But Hugh was firm. He knew he was right, and neither storms nor prayers would make him yield. So taking his little sister by the hand he bade good-by to his young friends, and hurried away.

Percy was wild at what he called "Hugh's

disgraceful conduct," and as the boy disappeared, his good resolutions vanished, and he went off in a whirl of passion to his room.

Frightened at the look of fierce anger in her brother's face, Theo crept away to her books and toys. She knew by experience that it was best to leave him alone till the storm should have subsided.

Percy shut himself in his room, and walked restlessly up and down. He was in a feverish state of rage and indignation. His will had been thwarted, his wishes treated lightly — without respect; and this by Hugh, whom he had liked so much, and to whom he had been so kind. Percy was not accustomed to such treatment, and he felt injured and insulted.

For some time all was silent. Theo took her luncheon, and went out with her governess; and still the boy remained in solitary confinement.

But at last, wild stormy peals from the organ filled the hall and passages, then fell by degrees into sad solemn tones, and finally faded away into sweet melodies, known and loved by Percy from his infancy. These his mother had sung to him as a child, with these she had soothed him in many an hour of bitter sorrow.

And now as they come forth from his touch, the form that he loved so passionately rose before him, and the dear face, saddened by his wickedness, seemed to rebuke him as he sat. His hands fell motionless by his side, his white lips quivered, and with an agonized cry of " mother, mother," he burst into tears. Long and bitterly he wept, till at last, tired and exhausted, he crept over to the fire, and laying his head against the sofa fell fast asleep.

It was late when he awoke, and shivering with cold groped his way to the door. It had grown quite dark, and as the fire had gone out whilst he slept, he had great difficulty in knowing which way to turn. At length, he reached the door, and drawing back the bolt passed out into the hall.

He was giddy and faint, for he had eaten nothing since his breakfast; but he felt ashamed to ask the servants for food at that hour, and resolved to wait till his father's dinner at eight o'clock.

Stealing quietly along through the hall, lest any one should hear him, he opened the library door and went in.

It was a large, handsome room; the walls were lined with rich paintings, the book-cases filled with valuable books; shaded lamps stood about on the tables, and a cheerful fire burnt in the grate.

Shutting the door softly, Percy looked cautiously around; then approaching the fire, he spread out his numbed fingers and gazed lovingly at a portrait of his mother that hung over the mantle-piece.

"Yes, mother," he whispered, "I have been wicked again—very wicked. But, oh! you know how much I have to bear, and how hard it is for me to be good. Mother, mother, when shall I grow patient and good-tempered? When shall I conquer this passion and anger, and become what your son ought to be?" And the tears ran down the boy's cheeks; for his mother's face seemed sad to him just then.

"What; all alone, Percy?" cried his father, entering the room at this moment. "Where is Theo?"

"I don't know where she is papa, but I"—

"Hullo, my little man, what's this? Crying again, I declare? Now, Percy, this won't do; you must really try to be happy. At your age, and with so many pleasant things about you, you should be as contented as possible."

"Yes, papa, I know I should; but I have

been angry and wicked to-day, and that always makes me unhappy."

"Angry and wicked, Percy? Why that sounds very dreadful," said his father, drawing the boy upon his knee. "Why have you been naughty? Has Theo been tormenting you?"

"No, no, papa; Theo has been very good; but you see I was angry with Hugh, and"—

"Angry with Hugh? Why, you seemed quite fond of him this morning. Surely he did not do anything to annoy you?"

"Well, you see, papa, he *would* go home," said Percy, sadly, "and I wanted him to stay and help me to be good, and he wouldn't, and"—

"And then you got cross, I suppose?" said his father gravely. "But Hugh was right to go. I am sure his mother wanted him; and, now, Percy, it seems to me you make too much fuss about being good. You want to be good, only in your own way, and I don't think that is right."

"No, papa; I'm afraid it's not."

"And I cannot understand how Hugh could help you. He's only a little boy, and"—

"But he's so good, papa, and talks so beautifully about God and heaven. And I do so want to be good and go to heaven to mamma—I do so want to go to her," cried Percy in a choking voice. "Hugh says I shall, if—if"—

"Hush, Percy, dear," said Sir Henry, with tears in his eyes, as he raised them from his weeping child to the face of his dead wife.

"You are good, and you shall go to her, of course; but not just yet, darling. I could not spare my little son—I should be very lonely without him."

"Would you really be sorry to lose me, papa? My cousins always say you would be glad to get rid of your hunchback son. Charlie Torrens says you wanted to adopt him."

"My poor lad. Did they really say such cruel things to you? But do not believe them, Percy; I would not give one curl of your golden hair for the whole lot of them. I did speak of adopting Charlie, but only in a business way — only with a view to his own interests. I thought of taking him into the office, and if he turned out well, of giving him a partnership. Then I wanted him to live here, and be a companion to you. He is your cousin, and I"—

"He could never be a companion for me, papa," cried Percy, vehemently. "He hates me, and loves to make me miserable. But, papa dear, Hugh is quite different. Hugh is good and gentle, and — oh, please, please adopt Hugh and make him my brother," and, turning round with a sudden jerk, Percy flung his arms round his father's neck.

"Your brother, Percy?" asked Sir Henry, smiling. "Would a cousin not be near enough, do you think?"

"Yes, yes," cried Percy; "cousin or brother, I don't much care which, so long as I can have him with me as much as I like."

"I am glad you like Hugh," said Sir Henry, "for he is, I think, a noble fellow. It is truly wonderful how he came to find that pocket-book."

"Still some one had to find it, papa."

"Yes, of course. But still it was extraordinary I should happen to drop it just where Hugh stood, and that he, of all people, should find it."

"Well, it was certainly very lucky, for that poor little crossing sweeper might have picked it up, and "—

"But that's just what did happen, dear. Hugh was the crossing sweeper, and he "—

"Oh, papa; why I thought Hugh was a gentleman?"

"And so he is, dear, as true a little gentleman as ever was born," said Sir Henry, warmly. "And, now Percy, in order to explain matters to you, I must tell you a story."

"About Hugh, papa?"

"Yes, partly about Hugh. But first about his parents."

"I shall be so glad to hear it, papa. Did you go to see Mrs. Brown to-day?"

"Yes, I went to see Mrs. Brown, Percy, and from her lips I heard the story I will now tell you. Some fifteen years ago she married Philip Brown and went to Australia. Her father was seriously displeased at her conduct, and cast her off completely. For some time the husband and wife lived happily enough in the bush; but at last Philip grew tired of the life there, sold his farm and went to Melbourne. But he was not long satisfied there either, so he made another change, and carried his family off to London. Longing for news of her father and sister (for her mother had died before her marriage), Mrs. Brown went to her father's office in the city, hoping and praying that time had softened his heart and lessened his anger.   But she found that he was dead — had been dead for some years. And his daughter? Could they tell her any news of his daughter, she asked. 'Yes; she had married — but was since dead.'   When I heard that my dear Theo was gone, I asked no more,' said Mrs. Brown, and "—

"Theo," cried Percy. "Why, that was mamma's name."

"Yes, Percy, so it was; and so I told Mrs. Brown, when she mentioned her sister's name."

"'Yes, I thought so,' she replied. 'When I saw the little packet of hair with the name and date, I felt certain that it belonged to the owner's dead wife. But, may I ask, Sir Henry, what was your wife's family name?'"

"Certainly," I answered; "my wife's name was Winter."

"'And my father,' she said, trembling with emotion, 'my father was Hugh Winter, of Mincing Lane.'"

"'Then, my dear Mrs. Brown,' I cried, 'I am your brother-in-law, for my wife was Theo Winter, youngest daughter of Hugh Winter, of Mincing Lane. You must be the sister whom she loved so well, and whose loss she mourned so long.'"

" 'Yes, I feel certain that I am your wife's sister. This is the likeness of my sweet Theo — is it at all like your dear wife?' and she handed me a pretty miniature which was, indeed, a true portrait of your mother."

" Why, then, papa, Hugh and I are really cousins?" cried Percy, with dancing eyes.

" Really cousins, my boy. So you see you have got your heart's desire."

" And I cannot tell you how glad I am. Dear, dear Hugh. How happy we shall be together. It is certainly strange how we came to find it all out. Now, I understand why you thought it wonderful that Hugh should pick up your pocket-book, papa."

" Yes, I thought you would," replied his father. " To me it seems the most extraordinary coincidence, that I should drop my valuable book at the feet of my wife's nephew, of whose existence I had not the faintest notion."

" It certainly was," said Percy, thoughtfully. " But is my aunt so very poor that she was obliged to send her son out to sweep a crossing? That is horrid work for a boy to do."

" So it is, and he shall never do it again,"
answered Sir Henry. " But his father had
been a long time without earning anything.
The expense of his illness had exhausted the
small sum that his wife had managed to save or
earn, and my poor sister-in-law was in despair.
They were literally without a penny and had
not a friend to go to. Then little Hugh came
to the rescue, and rushing off to the Strand,
was lucky enough to pick up a few shillings at
the crossing."

" Poor boy, it must have been disagreeable
work," said Percy, with a shudder. " But,
papa, we must never allow them to be so poor
again. They are our own dear relations; and
we have a right to help them."

" Most certainly we have, dear boy. I saw
poor Philip and had a long talk with him. I
told him that from this day he must look upon
me as his brother. If he gets well, I shall get
him as good a post in the city as he is capable
of filling. If he dies, his wife and children
shall become my special charge, and shall
never want for anything."

" Oh, papa, I am so glad you told him so,"
cried Percy. " But will my poor uncle die, do
you think?"

"It is hard to say, Percy. But he seemed very weak. That accident, that he met with in the street, has shaken him terribly. Then his heart is seriously involved. In fact, the doctors do not give any hope of his recovery."

"I am so sorry, for it will be a sad trouble for Hugh. He loves his father very dearly, and thinks him wonderfully clever."

"Poor fellow, perhaps he may be," said Sir Henry, sadly. "But, from what I have heard, he lacks perseverance and steadfastness of purpose. Without these virtues it is impossible for any man to get on, be he ever so talented."

"Poor man," said Percy. "But, oh, papa, wouldn't mamma have been glad to have seen my aunt and Hugh and Susie? Just think how happy it would have made her."

"Yes, indeed, it would, for she so often fretted over her absent sister. That thought would make us kind to them, even if we did not feel anxious to be so, for their own sakes."

"I should just think it would," cried Percy, eagerly. "But, papa, no one could know Hugh and Susie, without loving them at once. Oh, won't Theo be glad? Why, she was wild about Susie. I must run off now and tell her the good news."

As Percy ran out of the room calling for his sister, Sir Henry sighed, and leaning his arms upon the mantle-piece gazed earnestly at the portrait of his wife.

"My darling Theo," he murmured softly, "would that you had been here to welcome your sister and her children. How happy such a meeting would have made you. But I promise to do what I can to help them and make them comfortable. Hugh will be a companion for our poor afflicted son. He is frank and straightforward; his sunny temper will help our Percy to be bright and"—

"Papa, papa, here is Hugh come back, just when we wanted him," cried Percy, breaking in suddenly upon his father's reflections.

Sir Henry turned in surprise, and there stood Hugh, looking pale and anxious.

"And Hugh, did you hear that we are cousins after all?" cried Percy. "And you can come here as often as you like, and we shall have such fun; but, goodness, what is the matter? Why are you crying?"

"Oh, Percy, my"— and Hugh sobbed aloud.

"My dear boy, why do you weep?" asked Sir Henry. "Is anything wrong?"

"Oh, Sir Henry," sobbed Hugh, "my father is very ill — he is dying."

"Dying!" cried Sir Henry; "this is, indeed, bad news."

"Hugh, Hugh, I am so sorry," cried Percy. "Just when I found out we were cousins, and wanted to be so happy."

"Mother felt sure my father was getting well again, he seemed so bright after your visit, Sir Henry," said Hugh, in a choking voice. "But he is much worse this evening, and he is so anxious to see you again before he dies. I was sure you would come, so I ran off at once to — to " —

And poor Hugh broke down, weeping bitterly at the thoughts of losing his dear father so soon.

"This is a great trouble for you, dear Hugh," said Sir Henry, gently. "It is always hard to lose those we love. But do not despair; whilst there is life there is always hope. But, if your father should die, you must be brave and bear up for your mother's sake."

"Yes, I will do my best," said Hugh. "But, oh, what is to become of her and Susie? I am only a little boy, and cannot earn money enough to support them."

"But you are our cousins now," cried Percy; "and you know we have plenty of money, Hugh."

"Yes, Hugh, I am your uncle," said Sir Henry, putting his arm around the weeping boy, and drawing him towards him. "And as long as I live, neither you nor your mother shall be allowed to want. If your father dies I shall be a second father to you, and look after your interests, as if you were my own son."

"You are good — so good," cried Hugh, "and God was truly merciful to send you to us. But, please, uncle, do not delay any longer. Let us hurry away, for my poor father was so anxious to see you."

"I will go with you now, at once, dear boy," answered Sir Henry, starting to his feet. "Percy, you had better have something to eat, and go to bed. I may be very late, so do not think of waiting up for me."

"I will do whatever you wish, my own dear father," cried Percy, clinging to Sir Henry, and kissing him tenderly. "Good-night, Hugh — dear cousin Hugh. I do hope my uncle may get well again, for then we shall be all happy together."

Poor Hugh sobbed out a few words of thanks to his new cousin, bade him a tearful goodnight, and followed Sir Henry out of the room.

Percy took his father's advice, ate a hasty repast, and retired to bed. He was worn out with weeping and excitement, and soon dropped off into a deep refreshing sleep.

CHAPTER VII.

GREAT CHANGES FOR ALL.

PHILIP BROWN died next day, a happy, peaceful death. The poor man was reconciled to his fate, and quite content to go. He knew that his wife and children were in good hands, and he died blessing God for having sent them such a true friend as Sir Henry Randall. This was a sorrowful time for Hugh and his mother; but their grief was greatly softened by the kindness of their benefactor, and his warm-hearted children. Long and earnest were the consultations between Mrs. Brown and her brother-in-law, as to what was best to be done for the little family in the future.

Sir Henry most generously undertook their entire support, and settled a comfortable income upon Mrs. Brown for her life. Touched to the heart by so much kindness the good lady tried to thank him, and, with tears in her eyes, bade God bless him for his noble conduct. But Sir Henry only smiled, and assured her that he was but doing his duty.

"Your father was a wealthy man, dear friend," he said, "and, had you been living at home at his death, you would have received at least half the fortune that was left to my wife."

"Yes. That is, if I had never displeased him," she cried. "But, Henry, you know he died without forgiving me."

"Had you been near, I feel sure that forgiveness would have been yours, Lucy," he answered, gravely. "But, thank God, I have found you, and am able to restore the money that should have been yours many years ago."

"You are a noble fellow, Henry," cried the widow. "My children and I shall pray for you night and day."

"Thanks, dear sister; but do not let the thoughts of this money oppress you. Take it as your own, and do not praise me too loudly for doing my duty."

"I shall do as you wish," she answered, pressing his hand. "But you cannot prevent

me having my own thoughts about your goodness."

"No, I suppose not," he said laughing.
"But, now, when are you going to leave this
lodging and come to Holland Park? There
is plenty of room for you all."

"Many thanks, Henry; but, for various
reasons, I would rather stay where I am for
the present. I am not accustomed to such an
establishment as yours, and I would rather be
quiet for some months to come."

"I can quite understand that, dear," said Sir
Henry; "but poor Percy will be so terribly
disappointed. He is most anxious to have
Hugh with him. In fact, he would like to
have him to live with him, study with him,
and"—

"And would you like that arrangement?"

"Most certainly I would. It would be
splendid for Percy," said Sir Henry, earnestly.
"If you could bring yourself to spare Hugh,
it is what I should like above all things."

"Then, I see no reason why he should not
go to you. He can come to see me very
often, and it will make me happy to think
that I have been able to do you the smallest
service."

And so it was arranged, that after the first few weeks of mourning, Hugh was to take up his abode at Holland Park, whilst Susie and his mother remained in their lodgings till a pretty house could be taken and furnished for them in the neighborhood of Richmond.

Thus everything was comfortably settled, and, about a month after his father's death, Hugh went off with a light heart to begin a new life in his uncle's house.

The young Randalls were delighted at the thoughts of having their cousin always with them, and they did all they could to make his room look nice and pretty,

"I am so sorry he cannot have a room near mine," said Percy; "but as there is none, of course, he must go upstairs."

"The blue room looks very snug, now that we have put books and things about on the tables," replied Theo, "and I am sure Hugh will like it very much; but, do you know, Percy, I am afraid the servants will not be very polite to him. Just fancy Kapes wondering that we would give such a handsome room to a poor relation. Wasn't it impudent of her?"

"A poor relation, indeed!" cried Percy, indignantly. "How does she know whether he is poor or not?"

"Oh, Kapes knows everything," said Theo. "She asks so many questions and listens to our talks."

"Well, you are very silly to answer her questions. I don't think it's at all nice for a young lady to gossip so much with a servant. I wouldn't do it if I were you."

"But Kapes has been here so long. It seems quite natural to tell her everything, Percy."

"I think she has been here too long then; and if she doesn't take care, and mind her own business, papa will soon send her spinning."

"She doesn't believe that papa would ever send her away," said Theo, shaking her head. "She is a good servant, and has been here for so many years. But, oh, Percy, do you know what she has done? She wrote and told Aunt Lydia all about Hugh and Aunt Lucy. Won't she be in a rage?"

"Well, what if she is?" said Percy fiercely. "Aunt Lydia has no right to say a word. She ought to be glad that dear mamma's sister has been found again. And as for Hugh, I suppose papa can do what he likes in his own house!

He may ask who he likes to come here without her permission, I should think."

"Yes, of course, he can; but then Aunt
Lydia makes such a fuss, and I know she
makes papa unhappy with things she says.
She wanted him to adopt Charlie, and now she
will be angry when she hears about Hugh."

"I'm sure I hope she may," said Percy,
laughing. "Perhaps it will keep the whole
family from coming here to stay, and that
would be a blessing. But, listen, Theo, don't
you hear a cab? I'm sure I heard one stop.
Yes — so I did. Hurra, hurra, I'm sure it's
Hugh. I shall go out and meet him."

As Percy ran down the hall, a ring was
heard at the bell, and in a few minutes the
door was flung open, and Hugh entered the
house.

He was slightly flushed, and his voice
trembled nervously, as he asked the footman
to carry in his trunk.

"Hurra, hurra, there you are, my boy,"
cried Percy. "Welcome home, welcome
home."

And, at his cousin's cheery tones, Hugh's
embarrassment vanished, and he became his
own bright self again.

"Take that trunk up stairs, John," said Percy. "The blue room is to be Master Hugh's."

"Yes, Master Percy," answered the footman, respectfully, and shouldering the box he disappeared up the back-stairs.

"And now come along and see Theo. She thought it more dignified to receive you in state." And laughing merrily, Percy put his arm round Hugh, and led him away to his room.

There Theo awaited them, and running forward, she, too, welcomed Hugh with eager delight.

"You know this room, my boy," said Percy. "This is my own special sanctum, and it's a great favor to be allowed in here, I can tell you. Theo is sometimes bolted out of it for days; but that is when we fight; you and I will never fight, Hugh."

"I hope not," answered Hugh, gravely.

"I was sorry not to have you sleeping near me; but there was no room. I always sleep in this little nest," said Percy, and raising a crimson curtain he displayed a large alcove fitted up as a bedroom. "Papa likes me to stay here. He thinks it more convenient for me than running up and down stairs."

"Yes, I am sure it is," said Hugh. "And it all looks nice and comfortable."

"So it is, as snug as possible. Papa took great pains to get me every thing I wanted. He put up a bath, you see, quite close. Then, that thick curtain instead of a door, and that passage, which he always keeps filled with flowers, cuts me off from the rest of the house. I can lock the door at the end if I choose, and then no one can come near me."

"It is a regular little house all to yourself," said Hugh, smiling. "But what is this door?"

"That goes up the back-stairs, in case I wanted to run up quickly to papa's room at any time. I have a key for that, too; but come and let us have our tea, Hugh. You know this part of the world pretty well now. By-and-by I will show you your own little den."

The table was spread for tea, and the little Randalls were anxious to make their visitor partake of all the good things that they had set out in his honor. But Hugh was excited and strange, and had little appetite for anything.

"Was Susie sorry to part with you, Hugh?" asked Theo. "Did she want to come with you?"

"Yes, she was very sorry, poor darling,"

said Hugh, his eyes filling with tears. "But I promised to ask cousin Theo to have her to spend a day with her soon."

"Of course I will, the pet," cried Theo. "I wish aunt and she had come with you."

"Mamma did not care to do that for some time yet," and Hugh's tears fell fast.

"Oh, well, you must not fret, Hugh, dear," said Percy, kindly. "You will often see them both. When aunt is at Richmond we shall drive down to see her constantly; and after awhile she will come here."

"Yes, I know — I know," said Hugh, in a low voice. "But I never was away from my mother and sister before, and "—

"I am sure it is hard to leave them," cried Percy; "but still you must not be unhappy about it. They are not very far off, and you are with cousins who love you dearly. Come along and I will show you your room."

"It is quite ready," said Theo, "and I hope you will like it, Hugh. Percy and I arranged it ourselves this morning."

"You are both very good," answered Hugh. "I never thought you would be so good and kind."

"Don't praise us too much, Hugh," said

Percy, gayly. "Just wait a little before you decide about our goodness. You need not imagine that we are always as amiable as this. We shall torment you finely before you are very long with us, or I am greatly mistaken. But come up stairs with me now."

Hugh was in raptures with his room. He had never seen such a beautiful one before, and pinched himself several times to make sure that he was not dreaming.

The dainty pale blue hangings and pretty curtained bed were far too pretty, he thought; and he shouted with joy when he saw the bookcase full of choice books — the writing-desk with its exquisite contents.

Here he felt, no matter what occurred, no matter who was unkind to him, he could make himself perfectly happy.

Percy was much pleased with his cousin's evident delight, and told him that all the room contained was his own, to do exactly what he liked with.

Hugh thanked him again and again, and was so much overcome with gratitude and astonishment, that Percy thought it best to leave him to recover himself at his leisure.

"You will soon get accustomed to your

room and to us, Hugh, and you will find
that we are not half so pleasant as we look.
But good-night. Sleep well. We are to
begin our lessons to-morrow with Mr. Barker,
so you must be up early," and kissing his hand,
Percy shut the door, and ran down stairs.

In a very short time Hugh became quite
happy in his new home. He had every comfort that money could buy; was treated with
great kindness by his uncle and cousins; and
managed to spend many days and nights with
his darling mother and little sister.

Percy was rather hard to deal with at times;
but then he was always so sorry when he had
behaved badly, so penitent after a fit of passion, that Hugh could not feel vexed with him
long, and soon learned to love his poor deformed cousin with a strong affection.

Sir Henry had provided the boys with a
clever tutor, and they worked at their studies
with great eagerness and attention. Hugh was
far in advance of Percy, and was able to help
him to prepare his lessons. They both made
rapid progress, and Mr. Barker was well
pleased with his pupils.

Theo grew very fond of Hugh, and often
wondered what he had done to make Percy so

nice and good-tempered; whilst Sir Henry was truly thankful to him for bringing so much sunshine into his little son's life.

"It is really wonderful, Hugh, how the time passes now," said Percy, one day. "It used to creep over so slowly that a week seemed a long, tiresome time to go through."

"Ah, that was because you were idle," said Hugh, with a smile. "Now we have so much to do that the days pass quite quickly."

"I should just think they did," said Percy, laughing. "Why, I declare, I have hardly time to call my soul my own, between you and Mr. Barker. And do you know, Hugh, I have not been in a rage for a whole fortnight."

"So much the better," answered Hugh, gayly. "But I've got some good news for you. Mr. Barker is not coming this afternoon, so we can go where we like."

"How jolly," cried Percy. "Shall we go and see Aunt Lucy, and take Susie some chocolate creams?"

"No, thanks. I am going to see them on Sunday, and I saw them yesterday, so I think we might go somewhere else to-day."

"Where shall it be, then?"

"Well," said Hugh, gravely, "I should like

to go to the Children's Hospital, in Great Ormond Street."

" Oh, but "— said Percy, flushing, " there are so many strangers there — I "—

" You don't like strangers, I know," replied Hugh, gently. " But still, Percy, they are only poor, suffering little children. A boy I used to know is there, and I want to take him something. He broke his leg, poor chap, and has a good deal of pain to bear. Mother goes to see him very often, and he told her he was sure I would be too proud to visit him now."

" Too proud to visit whom, Hugh?" asked Theo, coming in at this moment.

" Too proud to visit no one, fair cousin," said Hugh, laughing. " But a fellow I know has broken his leg, and been carried to the hospital, and he thinks I am too grand now to go to see him."

" But you are not," said Theo, decidedly. " And I'm not. Let us all three go some day."

" I want to go to-day — now — but Percy "—

" Oh, Percy will come; it will be charming," cried Theo. " We'll take some oranges and cakes for the little ones. Say you'll come."

But Percy was lost in thought. It was

always an effort for him to meet strangers, so
conscious was he of his sad deformity.

"Hugh," he said, after a few moments'
reflection, "is it a good thing to visit these
sick children?   Does — does — God like us to
go?"

"Yes, indeed, He does, Percy. It will please
God very much, and will do us a great deal of
good."

"Then I will go," said Percy, and he turned
to get his hat.

"I must pack up a few things to take with
us," cried Theo, and off she flew to make her
preparations.

A few hours later the three children presented themselves at the door of the hospital
and were speedily admitted. They asked to
be taken to the accident ward, and were led
into a large room around which were ranged
a great many little beds.

The place looked bright and pleasant, and a
number of small heads were popped up from
the pillows to gaze at the visitors.

Hugh's friend was a boy of eight years old,
who had managed to break his leg a few weeks
before. But it was now almost mended, and
he was going home very soon.

"I'm sorry to go, for it's like heaven to be here," he said to Hugh, with a sigh. "But mother wants me badly to help her wid the young 'uns."

Percy wandered up and down, looking sad and perplexed. He glanced with pity at the little pale faces, but did not dare to speak to any one, and shrank away as though in pain, when a nurse passed him by.

But Theo was quite at home amongst the children, and set them all laughing about her, as she plied them with questions and good things.

"Percy," she cried, "come over here and look at this little fellow. See how cheerful and happy he is."

Percy went somewhat closer, and looked curiously at the boy, who had a pinched, thin face and a crooked, twisted back.

"He says his father was a Punch and Judy man," said Theo, "and that he used to go about with him and collect pennies after each performance. But he fell down stairs and broke his back, and the doctors say he will never be able to walk straight again."

"Poor little man," said Percy, softly, "and yet he can smile and look happy."

"Oh, yes; he says he doesn't mind much now. His father has promised to make him a cobbler—a man that mends shoes, you know."

"A pleasant look-out certainly," said Percy. "I can't think how he can look so cheerful—but he doesn't understand—he doesn't feel; he's only a baby."

"I'm not a baby," said the mite, in a shrill voice. "I'm six years old—and I know very well—but I don't mean to fret; for nurse says it was God let me fall; and He will always love me an' take care of me, an' mother says it will maybe keep me from wicked ways."

"You are a good little boy, and I'm sure God loves you very dearly," said Theo, and giving him a double supply of cakes she passed on to the next bed.

But this little one, a girl of nine, was frightened at her approach, and hid her head under the bed-clothes.

"She won't speak to me," said Theo to the nurse. "What is the matter with her?"

"Poor child, she is afraid of every one," answered the nurse. "She had a drunken father who beat her so dreadfully that he nearly frightened her out of her senses. She broke her leg, and her mother brought her here. Her father is dead since; so I hope she will be happier when she goes home again."

"I wish she would look up," said Theo. "I like to see the little things smile at me."

"Yes," said the nurse; "but I think that child has forgotten how to smile, she has had so much sorrow."

"Poor little girl," said Theo softly. "Oh, Percy, how happy we ought to be."

"Yes, I know; but come home, Theo. I don't like this place. It makes me feel ashamed to think how cross and discontented I am, and how good they are."

"Rich children are apt to forget to be thankful to God for all the good things He has given them," said the nurse, gently. "They grumble and complain about small trifles, and never remember those who are in real sorrow and distress."

"I will come again," said Theo, lingering to take a last look at her little favorite with the crooked back. "I will come again, for I love to hear them talk."

But Percy was impatient to be off, and calling to Hugh, he hurried him down stairs.

"I feel as though I should have cried had I stayed there any longer," he said to his cousin. "But from this day I will try my best not to complain because God has made me a hunchback."

"That is right," said Hugh, brightly. "For, indeed, indeed, it does not matter one bit."

CHAPTER VIII.

AN UNEXPECTED VISITOR.

SIR Henry Randall was an affectionate father, and desired nothing so much as the happiness of his children. But he was much occupied and greatly sought after, and so the little people were left very much to themselves. Many of his friends advised him to marry again, for he was young, handsome, and rich; but he loved the memory of his dead wife too dearly ever to think of putting another in her place. Others said he should have an elderly lady to look after his household and keep his children in order. This, again, was an idea that neither he nor his little ones approved of, and so they went on leading an independent life that shocked their friends and relations.

Sir Henry was the most indulgent of men. He rarely found fault with his children, and allowed them upon every occasion to do exactly as they pleased.

In this he was wrong, however. He loved his little ones and desired to see them happy; but he forgot that it is only by learning young to correct our faults and overcome our passions that we can ever hope for happiness in this world. Lessons in patience and self-denial are more precious than all the pleasures that wealth can buy. By them alone we are enabled to bear the troubles and afflictions that must come to each one of us in due time.

The truth of this, Percy and his father learned to their cost when the hour of temptation came round.

Meanwhile, things went on pleasantly, the children had their own way, were delighted with their new companion, and were extremely happy.

But the time of trial was at hand, although they knew it not.

One evening, about a week after the visit to the hospital, Hugh sat alone in Percy's room. The other children had gone to have a chat with their father, and he gladly took advantage of the quiet to enjoy a little reading.

But his peaceful enjoyment was of short duration, for very soon the curtain was plucked aside, and Percy and his sister came bounding across the room.

" Hugh, my old student," cried Percy gayly, " papa has just gone off to a dinner party, so wake up from your book, and let us have some fun."

" What shall we do?" asked Hugh, springing to his feet. " Shall we act charades? I've thought of such a splendid word."

" No, no, there are too few for charades to-night. It's better to have them when papa is here as audience."

" Poor Uncle Henry," said Hugh, laughing. " It's too bad to ask him to listen to our nonsense. It must bore him greatly."

" Not at all," said Percy. " So long as we are happy he is quite pleased."

" I know what we'll do," cried Theo. " Boys, it will be capital."

" What?" asked the boys.

" Let us turn out the gas all through the house and play ' Dark Forty.' "

" Splendid," cried Percy. " I'll hide my eyes, and you two run off. Turn out the gas as you go along. Here goes for this room." And in an instant they were all in the dark.

Away went Theo and Hugh racing and laughing. Out went the gas in passages and on stairs, and in a few minutes the big house was in complete darkness.

Then came Percy, groping his way up and down, till at last Theo was caught, and had to take her turn at counting forty, till the others were hidden.

What fun they had. Up the stairs and down again; into rooms and up on beds; banging doors and opening others stealthily. Such shrieks of laughter, such racing and jumping, till at last, hot and exhausted, they returned to Percy's room.

" I don't know when I enjoyed anything so much," said Percy, flinging himself on the sofa. " But I am hot."

" I should just think so," cried Hugh. " But I think a little light would be pleasant," and he sprang to turn up the gas.

" Let us rest ourselves now," said Theo, giving the fire a poke. " It will be very nice to have a long chat and a rest."

" Yes, jolly," said Percy; " but, I say, are you two aware that it's near Christmas?"

" Yes, in three weeks' time we'll have Christmas Day," said Hugh.

" We shall have such a pleasant one this

year," said Percy. "Just ourselves and a few friends of papa's."

"But I'm sure Charlie and Cecil will expect to be asked during the holidays," said Theo. "They always were before."

"They're a pair of cads," said Percy, "and I hate them both."

"Hush, Percy, you must not say that," said Hugh. "It's very wrong."

"Besides, they are your own cousins," said Theo. "They're not very nice, I must say; but still they are gentlemen."

"Not they," cried Percy. "They have been to Eton, and they dress well, but they swagger about too much to be gentlemen."

"Why, Percy, that was Charlie's favorite word, 'swagger.' Everything was 'swagger' with him. I wonder you say it when you think so little of him."

"Yes, but I always think of it when I mention his name. But you have no idea how disagreeable those fellows are, Hugh. The last time they were here they killed my dear old bat."

"Killed a bat," cried Hugh. "Why, I thought"—

"Perhaps you never saw one," said Percy;*

* See White's "Natural History of Selborne.'

" but I had a tame, long-eared bat for a long time. It used to eat flies out of my hand, and I was very fond of it. Those cruel fellows killed it."

" Well, I wasn't sorry for that, Percy," said Theo. " It was a disgusting creature. I used to hate to see it hanging up there by its heels."

" Heels! By its hind claws," cried Percy. " But you were very foolish not to like it. It was such a queer thing that I loved it."

" A great deal too queer for my taste," said Hugh, laughing. " There were numbers of them flying about our street, in the summer time, and we were dreadfully afraid of them. The chaps used to imitate their cry by scraping two keys together during school hours."

" That was capital," said Theo. " But I am sure the master was very angry."

" Well, no ; because he never knew who did it. He thought the bats were behaving badly. The poor man used to look up at the ceiling, and into all the corners of the room. But, of course, he never saw any bats."

" I shall try and get another next summer," said Percy. " I love queer things. They comfort me some way."

Theo and Hugh both laughed heartily at this, declaring he was a " very queer thing " himself. Upon this, Percy flung the cushion at Hugh's head. Hugh returned it with a merry laugh, and a scrimmage ensued, as a matter of course. Flushed and excited, his face lighted up with a radiant smile, Percy stood upon the sofa, the velvet cushion raised above his head, when suddenly the visitors' bell pealed loudly through the house.

" Some one for papa," he remarked, and sent the pillow flying at Hugh's merry face.

" Hush, Hugh — Percy, listen," cried Theo. " There is some fuss going on. Who can be calling at such an hour ? "

" It is a woman's voice," cried Hugh, quickly. " Could it be my mother ? Can any thing have happened ? "

" Nonsense, Hugh, old man. What could have happened ? " said Percy, soothingly ; " but, Theo, Theo—how dreadful ! It is Aunt Lydia, I am sure."

" Aunt Lydia, Percy ? Oh, I hope not. What in the world would bring her here now ? "

" Well, Aunt Lydia it is, any way," said Percy. " Don't you hear that little brute,

Spark, barking? And listen, there is Mary Ann's shrill, squeaking voice."

" Oh, dear, oh, dear," sighed Theo. " Why does she come here now? Just when we are all so happy together. What shall we do? What shall we do?"

" Hide," cried Percy. " Oh, how I wish I had locked the door. Hugh — Theo — here she comes. Run under the sofa, Theo. Hugh and I will creep into my bed," and, lifting the curtain, Percy disappeared into the alcove, dragging Hugh along with him.

But Theo remained standing in the middle of the room. She did not care to double herself up in an uncomfortable position for dear knows how long, and was meditating a flight up the back stairs, when she felt herself seized by the arm and turned suddenly round to face the angry looks of her indignant aunt.

" Well, upon my word, this is a nice way to receive a visitor, and your own father's sister," cried the angry lady. " The whole house in darkness, and not a fire anywhere, till I find my way into this den."

" But we did not expect you, Aunt Lydia. We were playing ' Dark Forty,' and so we turned out the gas all over the place," and

Theo wriggled away from her aunt as fast as she could.

"Dear me, what a rude child you are," she cried, sinking down on the sofa; "and is this the way you behave yourselves in the evenings? Making a common play-ground of your father's beautiful house."

"Yes, of course," said Theo, tossing her head. "Papa does not mind. He lets us do exactly what we like."

"Humph, does he, indeed? Then, more fool he," and the lady gave a grunt of extreme dissatisfaction.

Mrs. Torrens was a tall, straight woman, with a thin, sharp face, pale complexion, and small but piercing gray eyes; her hair, of a dull drab, fell in thick ringlets on her shoulders, giving her the appearance of an antiquated old maid. Her figure, however, was very commanding; her dress rich and fashionably made.

This unwelcome visitor was Sir Henry Randall's only sister, and his senior by five years. She was one of those persons who like to manage everything and every one in her own particular way. And so, from time to time, she was in the habit of invading her brother's house, and trying to lay down the law for him and his children. For so far she had met with but little success, and had managed to make herself disliked by the whole household.

"Where is your brother, Theo?" she asked, sharply. "This is his room. Why isn't he visible, I'd like to know? The servants told me he was here."

"Percy has gone to bed, aunt," said Theo, trying hard to keep from laughing. "You see he did not know you were coming to-night."

"Neither did I, Miss Pert," snapped Mrs. Torrens, opening her eyes in a jerky manner. "But when I heard what was going on, I had to come to put a stop to it at once."

"Going on?" said Theo, in surprise. "Why there is nothing going on here, Aunt Lydia, I assure you."

"Nothing going on, indeed," replied her aunt, indignantly. "Then what does my brother mean by bringing in a beggar boy to live with his son and daughter? Do you call it nothing, that a low-born creature like that should pass his days with you and your brother?"

"But Hugh is not low-born, Aunt Lydia. He is our cousin, and " —

"Cousin, indeed," sneered the lady. "You

are not going to make me believe that story. It was easy for such adventurers to say, ' we are your relations '— for the mother to say her name was Winter. But that my brother should believe it all is what astonishes and angers me. As for the boy "—

" How dare you come here to insult my aunt and cousin, Aunt Lydia? How dare you find fault with my father's behavior?" cried Percy, as, pale and trembling with rage, he stood before Mrs. Torrens.

" Ho, ho! So you are not in bed after all, my most polite young nephew? Hiding behind curtains and listening to what is being said. That is what comes of having low companions."

" Leave my room, if you please," cried Percy, choking with passion. " I do not want you here — I "—

But Hugh's hand was laid upon his mouth, and Hugh's voice whispered in his ear:

" Hush, Percy. Do not be rude, dear boy. It is not right to speak so to a lady."

" Dear, dear. So there you are," cried Mrs. Torrens, with a sneer. " The clever adventurer who has made his way into this most trusting family, taken my Charlie's place, and robbed my boy of "—

"No, no, Lydia," said Sir Henry, who entered the room at this moment. "Your son has been wronged by no one but himself. He proved himself idle and conceited, and so I did not care to have him. He wished to become rich, but without any trouble or hard work. As for Hugh, you are very wrong to think him an adventurer. I have had proof — ample proof — that his mother is my dear wife's sister, and he her nephew. He is a good, truthful boy, and for that reason I am glad that Percy should have such a cousin to be his friend and companion."

"A very fine speech, upon my word, Henry," she cried. "But I am not so confiding as you are, and cannot believe in such a wild story. Why you should go out of your way to hunt for your wife's relations when you have plenty of your own, I can't imagine."

"I did not go out of my way, Lydia; but I am very thankful that I found Hugh and his dear mother before it was too late. I will tell you the whole story, show you the many proofs I possess, and"—

"Oh, I have heard the wonderful story, thank you, and on very good authority too."

"Kapes," whispered Theo to Percy, "she's at the bottom of all this."

"Well, then, I must ask you to say no more, Lydia," said Sir Henry, sternly. "Mary Ann says your room is ready, so I must ask you to leave the children to themselves."

"Oh, very well. I will say no more for the present," and picking up her little snarling pug, she sailed out of the room.

"And now, my friends, you had better go to bed," said Sir Henry to the children. "Be patient for a few days, and then your aunt will go away."

"I'll take good care she doesn't stay long," grumbled Percy. "I will make her as uncomfortable as ever I can. See if I don't. Why couldn't she have stayed at home?"

"Come, now, Percy lad, don't take her visit so much to heart," said his father, soothingly. "Go to bed, and forget that she is here."

"That's easier said than done, papa," cried Percy. "But I'll do my best to forget her, never fear; and I do hope she'll stay out of my room."

"We must try and make her do that, dear," replied Sir Henry. "But I don't think she will be likely to trouble you. She will have no business down here."

"But she'll make some," said Percy. "There never was such a person for poking as my respected aunt, Mrs. Torrens."

"Well, dear, you must bear with her for a time," said Sir Henry, and kissing his children, he bade them good-night.

"But, indeed, I wish Lydia had stayed at home," he said, as he shut himself into his room. "Percy and she could never agree. The poor fellow was getting so happy, and now I'm afraid she will make us all discontented whilst she remains amongst us. How terribly jealous she is about Hugh. Just as if her Charlie could ever have found the place in our hearts that that dear lad has taken. Well, I do hope her visit may be a short one. I cannot ask my own sister to go; but when she does, I shall not be sorry."

CHAPTER IX.

AUNT LYDIA SEES A GHOST.

THE angel of peace seemed to have flown away at Aunt Lydia's approach, and all Percy's good resolutions had taken their departure with him.

Between the boy and his aunt there was continual warfare; for Percy, hot and passionate as he was, could not listen quietly to her ill-natured remarks about his cousin. The very sight of her going about the house, the mere sound of her harsh voice, seemed to rouse all that was bad in his sadly undisciplined nature.

To Theo, who was pretty and graceful, Mrs. Torrens was kind and attentive. But to Percy and the " little adventurer," as she insisted on calling Hugh, her manner was most insulting.

Sir Henry and his sister were never altogether happy in each other's company. for they had but few interests in common. So seeing that her visit was likely to be a long one, he suddenly found it necessary to go off to the country on business. Percy was in despair at his father's departure, and felt certain that Mrs. Torrens would annoy him more than ever, since there was now no one by to protect him from her wrath.

But in this he was mistaken, and to his surprise Hugh and he were left to their own devices.

Mrs. Torrens was delighted when her brother went away; and taking advantage of his absence sent out invitations to her friends. After this, she seemed to forget the boys' existence, and troubled them little, so long as they remained in their own part of the house. This, they took care to do, and so the battles between nephew and aunt became less. frequent, as they seldom met.

Theo, too, they saw only at rare intervals. Her light little head seemed completely turned; and in the midst of the gayeties that were going on, she scarcely ever found time to visit Percy's room.

At first, the boys were much pleased at the new state of affairs, and between their lessons and games the days passed pleasantly enough.

But as time went on, and his father did not return, Percy began to mope about in a miserable way. By degrees his bad spirits developed into bad temper, and he became so cross and irritable, that Hugh had a hard time of it, and found it impossible to please him, in anything he did or said.

Then very soon everything went wrong, and even Hugh's bright face became clouded; he could not make his friend happy, and so he grew depressed and wretched himself.

At lesson time, Percy became wild and unmanageable, would learn nothing, and prevented his companions from doing their work, by his noisy, restless interference.

Their tutor was a quiet, amiable man, and did all he could to soothe the boy, but without effect, and at last stung by his insolent manner, he flung down the books and left the house, declaring that he would have no more to do with such an unruly pupil.

" Percy, Percy, what have you done?" cried Hugh; "do please let me call Mr. Barker back again. He will soon forgive you, if you say you are sorry."

" Nonsense, Hugh," replied Percy, angrily. " Call him back again, indeed; no fear of that,

old boy; I'm only too glad to see him disappear, I can tell you."

" But, Percy, you behaved very badly and
vexed him greatly. He says he will never
come back to teach us. I did not think you
could have treated him like that, for he has
always been so kind and "—

" Can't you leave a fellow in peace, Hugh?
You're a perfect worry, and if you go on
preaching at me, I'll shy this ink-pot at your
head. But don't you fret. Old Barker will
come back, never fear; and I'm jolly glad to
get rid of his jawing for this evening."

" Jawing, indeed," cried Hugh, indignantly.
" His lessons are most interesting."

" Yes, when a fellow's in the humor for
them. But those evening lessons were all your
doing, and I am sick of them. A chap can't
go on working forever. And I can tell you,
Barker was fine and cross to-night. I never
saw the like of him."

" You do well to talk about crossness," said
Hugh, hotly. " You were as insolent as ever
you could be; and I hope you will beg his
pardon if he does come to-morrow."

" Well, if you won't stop when you're told,"
cried Percy, with crimson cheeks and flashing

eye, " take that," and seizing a large cut-glass ink-bottle, he hurled it at Hugh's head.

But, fortunately, the boy saw it coming, and stooping quickly, escaped the blow which would have felled him to the ground had he not managed to avoid it.

Just behind Hugh stood a rare old cabinet, filled with curiosities, that had belonged to Percy's mother, and so ranked amongst his most sacred treasures. And now this bottle, aimed by his own hand, went crashing over his cousin's head, straight through the thick glass doors; and to his horror he saw the ink streaming over the crimson velvet shelves, spoiling the treasures that nothing could replace.

" Oh, Percy, Percy, they are all destroyed," cried Hugh, forgetting his own danger in his anxiety for the beautiful things. " Get the sponge quickly, and I'll try to soak up the ink, before it does much harm."

But Percy made no reply. The hot, red color of passion died away, leaving him deathly pale, as he gazed at the sad wreck of his beloved cabinet.

" Never mind, old man," said Hugh, gently. " It is not as bad as it looks. The glass is broken; but there are lots of things that we

can wash, and they'll look all right again.
The velvet can be replaced and the glass too;
so don't fret about it — there' a good fellow."

"Oh, Hugh, Hugh," whispered Percy, "I'm
so bad — so wicked; God ought to strike me
dead.   He ought to "—

"Hush, Percy; don't say that.   God is too
merciful to strike you when you are in a fit
of passion; but, oh, tell Him you are sorry —
beg Him to forgive you."

"But, Hugh, Hugh, if that bottle had killed
you, what should I have done; and if it had
hit you — oh, I dare not think of it.   That is
twice, Hugh, twice in such a short time, that I
have been so passionate — so wicked.   Oh,
what shall I do?   What shall I do?" cried
Percy, shuddering; and, bowing his head, he
wept bitterly.

"Thank God, it did not touch me, Percy.
But do not give way to despair.   You are passionate, and sometimes do dreadful things; but
you will be able to get over all that, if you
just fight against your temper like a man, and
pray hard — hard.   But, cheer up now, old
man, and let us see what we can do to make
these things look nice again."

Springing to his feet, Hugh hurried into

Percy's alcove, and coming back armed with a sponge and some water, began to soak up the ink with great care.

But Percy would not cheer up, as his cousin advised him to do, and sat upon the floor looking gloomy and miserable. He was so much overcome with grief and contrition, that even the thought of saving his treasures had not the power to move him.

Meanwhile, Hugh worked steadily on, and was rejoicing to himself that so many of the curious things were quite untouched, when the crimson curtain was suddenly raised, and Theo, radiant in all the glory of a pale blue ball dress, came bounding into the room.

" Now, then, you two poor hermits," she cried, gayly, turning herself round to be admired. " What do you think of my —? But, what can have happened? Hugh tell me what — oh! what smashed poor mamma's cabinet?"

But Hugh only flushed hotly at her questions, not knowing what to answer; he loved the truth, and yet would gladly have screened poor Percy.

"Oh, dear it is such a pity," said Theo, with tears in her eyes. "Poor mamma's cabinet,

that we all loved so dearly. I wonder you
are not ashamed of yourself, Percy. For, of
course, you must have done it in one of your
tantrums. It's quite true what Aunt Lydia
says : you are a very ill-tempered, bad boy,
and"—

This was too much for Percy, so, jumping
up, he seized her roughly by the arm, dragged
her across the room, down the passage, and
into the hall. Then, with a bang that re-
echoed through the house, he slammed the
door, locked it, and flinging the key upon
a table, sank with a groan into a corner of
the sofa.

"You are a cross, rude boy," cried Theo,
through the key-hole. "That's the thanks I
get for dressing early, and coming to tell you
about the ball to-night. The rooms and hall
look lovely, and I wanted you and Hugh to
come and see them. But you are so disagreeable and horrid; but, there, I shan't talk to
you any more." And she ran lightly away to
the drawing-room.

With great patience Hugh worked on at the
cabinet, and, at last, succeeded in washing the
ink stains off nearly all the valuable articles
that it contained. But when he turned in

triumph to show his handiwork to Percy, he would not deign to look at it, and did not reward him with a word of thanks.

The evening passed over in silence, and at last, feeling sad and dispirited, Hugh bade good-night to his cousin and went up stairs to his own room.

Percy did not seem to notice his departure, and sat staring into the fire, the look of gloom growing deeper and deeper as time went on.

Suddenly, the sound of a beautiful waltz comes floating through the room, and Percy listens eagerly, straining every nerve, so that he may catch each note of the music.

Forgetting all his misery, in his delight in the melodious sounds, he springs to his feet, smoothes his hair, pulls straight the lace collar at his neck, and seizing the keys that he had thrown aside in anger, walks quickly down the passage that leads to the large front hall.

The music has ceased ere he reaches the door; but he opens it a little, and peeps out to see what is going on.

The hall is filled with gayly dressed people, laughing and chatting as they walk up and down. One couple, a bright-looking girl and a tall, dark man, saunter up close to where

Percy stands concealed, and, unconscious of his presence, continue their conversation.

"What a pretty child Theo Randall is," remarks the young lady. And from his hiding place Percy sees his sister flitting about amongst the company.

"Yes; she is very pretty—a charming little girl," answers the gentleman, smiling. "But has not Sir Henry Randall a son? Why is he not here to-night?"

"Yes; he has a son," and the girl lowers her voice to a whisper. "But he is deformed—a regular hunchback I hear." Poor Percy shudders; the words cut him like a knife. "Mrs. Torrens says he is a frightful creature—quite too hideous to be produced."

"That is not true, and Mrs. Torrens is most unkind. Look at me and tell me that it is not true," cries Percy, as, quivering with rage, he flings open the door, and stands, with flashing eyes before his astonished auditors.

The gentleman starts round, eyes the boy curiously, and murmuring, "Poor little fellow," turns away with a sigh.

The young girl draws back for an instant, frightened at this sudden attack; but one glance at the white face, the golden hair, and beautiful eyes, tells her how wronged he has been, how unhappy her foolish words have made him; and stepping forward she gently kisses him on the forehead.

"It is, indeed, untrue, dear boy," she whispers. "But forgive my unkind speech. I did not know what I was talking about. But why are you not at the ball? Why are you hiding away by yourself down here?"

"Because I am not wanted," said Percy, bitterly. "Because — because," then feeling the tears coming into his eyes, he shook himself away from her, and rushed down the passage to his room. The kind-hearted girl would have followed him, but the door was shut in her face; so, feeling very sad, she took her partner's arm, and returned with him to the dancing room.

"Oh, how cruel Aunt Lydia is to say such things of me," cried Percy, in a whirl of passion, flinging his things here and there about the place. "Could she not leave me alone? Why should she talk of me in such a way to strangers? Oh, if papa only knew, he would be so angry — he would. Why should she make my deformity a subject of conversation? But I'll be revenged. I'll pay her off.

She shall have no peace of her life till she leaves this house; and that will be very soon, if I can manage it. I'll do something to get rid of her. I'll frighten her out of her senses — this very night, too. I'll be revenged; I must — I will."

The clock on the mantle-piece struck twelve, then one; and still Percy sat on, brooding over his unhappy fate and cruel treatment. "I'll do it — I'll do it," he cried, suddenly; and, seizing a candle, lighted it, and crept stealthily on to the back stairs, and passed silently up through the house.

The ball is over, the dancing at an end, and as the last carriage rolls away from the door, Mrs. Torrens seeks her chamber for the night.

The entertainment has been a success; and many compliments have been paid to the hostess by the departing guests. But even this has failed to make her happy, and a heavy cloud seems to hang over her, as she flings herself into an arm-chair by the fire. Her thin lips are set in hard lines, her brow wrinkled with some angry thought, and her voice sounds harsh and grating, as she orders her maid to leave her at once.

Very quickly Mary Ann removes the rich

ball dress, and places a warm dressing-gown round the lady's shoulders. Then taking the flashing jewels from her neck and arms, she packs them carefully away in their cases, and hurries from the room.

With a sigh of relief at finding herself alone at last, Mrs. Torrens draws forth a letter, and the look of anger deepens in her eyes, as she reads the short note over and over again.

But presently the letter drops from her fingers, and she falls into a restless sleep.

Suddenly, she awakes with a start, and looks nervously round the room. The fire has gone out, the candles have burnt low, and she shivers and draws her dressing-gown more closely about her, as she nestles back amongst the velvet cushions.

A rustling noise in a distant corner once more disturbs her, and fills her with alarm; then, again, all is quiet, and she closes her eyes with a sigh.

" How nervous I am," she murmurs. " It is only the wind. I feel strangely frightened, and yet, why should I? There is nothing to fear."

But, even as she speaks, the door of the large wardrobe opens slowly, and a tall, white figure glides across the floor to where she sits pale and terrified.

She starts quickly to her feet, but the room seems to whirl round, and the cold perspiration stands in great drops upon her brow, as this strange visitor comes silently towards her.

Raising her hand, Mrs. Torrens tries to ward off the coming danger; she strives to speak, but her voice is thick and muffled, her tongue dry and parched; and still the awful figure moves slowly, but surely, in her direction.

Making a frantic effort, the frightened woman rushes towards the door; but ere she can reach it, the mysterious visitor glides before it, and with one uplifted arm seems to forbid her approach.

Then the poor lady's strength and courage fail her, and with a wild shriek she falls senseless to the ground.

"Oh, she is dead! She is dead! I did not mean to kill her," cries the ghost; and letting the white sheet in which he had enveloped himself, drop from his face and head, Percy Randall runs screaming from the room.

CHAPTER X.

GOOD RESOLUTIONS.

WHEN Hugh said good-night to Percy, he went sadly up stairs to his own little room. He felt very unhappy, and a great longing came over him to run away from his troublesome cousin, and return to his darling mother.

He remembered with regret the peaceful, pleasant days he had spent in their humble lodging, and he felt inclined to go off, late and all as it was, and throw himself into his mother's loving arms. But then, he thought of his uncle's kindness, of poor Percy's affection, and his own great happiness before this cloud had come down upon them; and he resolved to be brave, bear his trials as patiently as possible, and do all he could to help his cousin to recover his good spirits.

Then, kneeling by his bedside, he prayed

long and fervently. He implored God to make him good and patient, and asked him to help Percy to conquer his dreadful passion, which was the cause of so much misery to them all.

After this he went to bed; but, alas, not to sleep. The whole house was filled with gay music from the ball-room, and the poor boy lay tossing about from side to side, wishing he could shut out the happy sounds which were so little in accordance with his own miserable thoughts.

All things have an end, however, even balls; and, to Hugh's delight, the last waltz was played, the last good-night was spoken; and, with a sigh of relief, he turned once more upon his pillow, and fell asleep.

But his rest was light and broken. Strange dreams haunted and troubled him, filling him with terror, and causing him to start up and gaze wildly into the dark corners of his room.

In all these dreams he found himself with Percy, exposed to some terrible danger, from which he struggled with all his strength to rescue his cousin, who clung to him, imploring him to help him—to—to save him.

"Yes, Percy, I will—I will," he cried, starting up and looking around him in alarm.

"Help me, Hugh; pray help me and tell me what I shall do," whispered a voice in his ear, and there stood Percy, with a white, scared look upon his face.

"Yes—but—why? What is the matter?" asked Hugh, now thoroughly awake. "Why do you look so strange and frightened, Percy?"

"Oh, Hugh, I have killed her," said his cousin, in a hoarse, choking voice. "She is dead—dropped in an instant at my feet. I am a murderer—I hated her—and I wanted to frighten her; but—but—I never meant to kill her."

"Never meant to kill who, Percy? Are you dreaming, dear, that you talk so wildly?" cried Hugh, seizing his cousin's hands, which were as cold as ice.

"I am not dreaming—I am wide awake. And, oh, Hugh, she is dead."

"Who is dead? What am I to do? Speak, and tell me. Who is it that is dead?"

"Aunt Lydia—Aunt Lydia," gasped Percy. "Be quick, and go to her room, and see. I wanted to make her nervous, and—and I dressed up as a ghost; and then when she saw me she fell—dead—and"—

But Hugh was gone; and soon Percy heard

him calling and shouting to Mary Ann, to get up and come to her mistress at once.

Doors opened and shut violently; lights appeared here and there through the house; voices were heard whispering at every corner, as the terrified servants came hurrying from their chambers.

Down on the floor in Hugh's room crouched Percy, his thin hands clasped tightly together in a perfect agony of despair.

But suddenly a sound fell upon his ear that caused his heart to beat wildly, and drove the unhappy look from his face. A sound that had once been the most hated he could hear, but which seemed to him now as sweet music, for it brought back hope to his mind, and drove away the maddening horror that had taken possession of his soul.

It was the sharp voice of his aunt that came ringing across the corridor, and filled him with joy, for it told him that she was alive, and that he was no murderer.

"Poor Percy, poor Percy," said Hugh, stealing back into his room, and putting his arm around his unhappy cousin. "Mrs. Torrens had only fainted, and she is quite well now; but how could you play such a cruel trick?"

"I know it was wrong and wicked," sobbed Percy; "but I wanted to be revenged, and"—

"Hush, hush," cried Hugh; "you should never try to be revenged on any one. We must leave that to God, Percy, and bear our troubles manfully; but come down now, and go to bed. You are trembling with cold, and I am afraid you will be ill to-morrow. And now you must really try and forgive Aunt Lydia, more than ever after to-night. She is very angry with you; but you must try and be patient, no matter what she says, for you have acted shamefully towards her. You expect God to love you, and forgive you your sins, and yet you cannot forgive her, for saying harsh things to you."

"And cruel things of me. Oh, if you had heard what I did to-night, you would know why I hate and detest her." And he told Hugh the conversation he had overheard between the young lady and her partner.

"Well, it was very hard to bear, Percy, I confess; but remember, listeners never hear good of themselves," said Hugh, "and now, you have put yourself in the wrong, by behaving so wickedly to Mrs. Torrens. If you are not prepared to be quiet and gentle with

her when you meet, I do not know what may
happen."

' I know I have been wicked," said Percy,
tearfully, " and I will try to forgive her ; but,
oh, it is hard — very hard."

The poor boy was completely worn out with
cold and excitement, so Hugh hurried him off
down stairs. He tucked him snugly up in bed,
bade him a kind good-night, and returned to
his own room, where, tired and exhausted, he
soon slept the deep, refreshing sleep of childhood.

Next morning both the boys looked pale and
weary, after the miserable experiences of the
night before.

Percy was sad and downcast, yet strangely
agitated and uneasy. Every time the door
opened, he trembled lest his aunt should appear
before him to upbraid him for his wicked conduct. He felt he had merited her wrath ; but
he dreaded the coming storm, and shuddered
as he thought of the bitter things she would
probably say to him.

Hugh noticed the anxious glances, the quick,
nervous manner, and guessing what was wrong,
resolved to save the poor boy for at least a few
hours longer.

"I tell you what, Percy," he said, trying to speak cheerfully, "it seems to me that we are both very miserable; so what do you say to our taking the pony carriage and going off somewhere? Mr. Barker does not seem to be coming to-day."

"No; I suppose he is too much offended to come after last night," said Percy, dolefully.

"Well, then, let us take advantage of our holiday and go somewhere."

"Very well, if you care to; but"—

"Oh, never mind buts, old man," cried Hugh, briskly. "See, there is a lovely frost. The ponies were roughed yesterday I know, so we'll go off somewhere for a drive. It will be very jolly and pleasant. Cheer up, my boy, and come along."

"Well, let us go to see Aunt Lucy and Susie. I have not seen them for such a long time; it is a capital drive to Richmond."

"By all means, let us visit Mrs. Brown in her new house," said Hugh, gayly. "I'm rather anxious to see how the furnishing is getting on."

"So am I," cried Percy, brightening. "I will ring and order the carriage at once."

It was just eleven o'clock, as the two boys

got into the pretty phaeton that Percy's kind father had provided for his little son's special use. Aunt Lydia had not yet appeared, and they drove off, feeling thankful at having escaped so well, and very joyful at leaving her and her hard words behind, even though it were only for a short time.

The day was cold and frosty, but the sun shone out bravely for December, and, as they were warmly rolled up in fur rugs, the sharp air touching their pale cheeks only made them glow and tingle, bringing brightness to their eyes and smiles to their lips.

Hugh was soon in high spirits, and the misery of the night faded quickly from his memory. He chatted away so merrily that even Percy grew more cheerful as he listened to his stories. And, at last, the fresh air and pleasant society did their work, and he became as lively as his cousin, joining heartily in his fun and laughter.

When the phaeton stopped at "Ivy Cottage," Mrs. Brown was sitting at the dining-room window sewing. She looked up at the sound of wheels upon the gravel, and, uttering a cry of joy, ran out to the door, and clasped her son in her arms.

"Here's an unexpected treat for you, mother," cried Hugh. "Percy and I were tired of town, so we thought we would just pop down and see how you are getting on."

"You are dear, good boys to think of me, and I am very glad to see you both," said Mrs. Brown, and she turned to kiss her little nephew. "I hope you are well, Percy; but why did Theo not come with you?"

"Oh, Theo was in bed when we came out, I believe," said Hugh, laughing. "The young lady was at a ball last night."

"A ball?" said his mother. "She is rather young for balls, surely!"

"It was at home," said Percy, frowning. "Papa was away, and my aunt, Mrs. Torrens, gave a ball."

"Indeed, I was not aware that she was at Holland Park still," said Mrs. Brown, gravely. "But, Hugh, dear, Susie will be sorry not to see you."

"Not see us, mother? Why shouldn't she, the darling? Where is she?"

"She has gone into the park to see the skating. Some little friends, with their nurse, called for her, and I don't expect her back for a long time."

"But we are going to spend the whole day with you, mother; that is, if you don't mind. We have a holiday, and thought we should like to give you the pleasure of our company."

"My dear Hugh, I am delighted. I have many little things to show you; and then Susie will see you, poor pet."

"All right, mother mine. We'll start off to the park and bring her home. But first give us some bread and cheese, for we are as hungry as hawks. Eh, Percy?"

"More hungry than I could ever tell you," answered Percy, laughing. "I think I could eat paving stones."

"Oh, mother won't ask you to do that," said Hugh, brightly, as the servant entered, bearing the luncheon tray. "Why, I declare, things go like clock-work in your little home," he cried, laughing. "I suggest bread and cheese, and, *presto*, it is here."

"Well, you see, Mary was bringing it in for me," replied his mother, with a smile, "and seeing visitors, she added a few things."

"Mary is a wise girl," said Hugh. "Come, Percy lad, come and refresh yourself. Here is some excellent bread, and some delicious milk, just to keep you going till dinner-time."

"What time would you like dinner, Hugh?" asked his mother.

"About four, I think; for we must get back at a reasonable hour this evening."

"Very well, then. I must go and order a few good things for you. I"—

"Muver, muver, open de door. Quit— quit. Tommy White says Hoo's here. Let me in quit, quit," cried a sweet, childish voice; and as the door was thrown open, little Susie came bounding into the room.

Flinging her arms round her brother's neck, she kissed and hugged him, till at length, laughing and breathless, the boy cried for mercy. Then she darted across to Percy, whom she knew very little, but loved dearly, because he was her darling Hugh's best friend.

"Cousin Percy, I love you—I love you," she cried, her face radiant with smiles. "You brought my own Hoo to see us, and, indeed, indeed, you is a wegy dood boy. Muver says we ought to love you, and I do—indeed I do."

"You sweet little thing," exclaimed Percy, taking her up on his knee, and covering her with kisses. "What a lucky chap you are to have such a dear, good-hearted sister."

"Yes, indeed," said Hugh, laughing. "She's not a bad mite, and she loves her brother dearly. Eh, old lady? But some folks would think Theo Randall more of a sister to be proud of than poor wee Susie Brown," and he tossed the small child high in the air.

"Oh, Theo is well enough to look at," said Percy. "I believe most people think her very pretty and all that kind of thing. But she doesn't care for any one — at least she doesn't love me as"—

"Now, Percy, that's not true," cried Hugh. "Theo loves you dearly, you know right well; but you"—

"Of course it's always my fault. [illegible] me," cried Percy, with [illegible] sister by the hand [illegible] you, Theo is cross a[illegible]hine, his face [illegible] forget the way she spoke to [illegible] Why she cares no more for me than for — for"—

"Now, Percy, that is not true," said Hugh, quickly. "You were very rude to her yesterday evening, when she came in so kindly to tell us about the ball. Theo is loving and good, and I think you should really be ashamed to speak in such a way about your sister. I'm very glad my mother has left the room. I should not like her to hear you say such things."

"What a lot of rubbish you can talk, to be sure. Perhaps if you knew Theo as well as I do, you "—

"And so I do. Just as well as you do, and much better," cried Hugh, warmly. "She is kind and loving, sweet-tempered and gentle. You give way to your passionate fits, and then you sulk over them till you think every one as cross as you are yourself."

"Thank you," said Percy, bitterly. "You are very kind. I am very fortunate "—

"No, I am not kind at all. But I think you ought to be just. You ought to remember "—

"He had all, I don't want to be preached who are always so go a list of Theo's virtues either. no. I am got to come and torment me last night, when I was in a rage, so you need not preach."

"I'm not going to preach, Percy, but I must say I "—

"Hugh, Hugh, come and see the skating," cried Susie, pulling him by the jacket. "It is lovely out in the park. And I am sure you and Percy would like it so much. Do come like good boys."

"What do you say, Percy?" asked Hugh. "Shall we go with the little one or not? It would do you good to go on the ice and see the fun. I brought a couple of pairs of skates, and I could teach you."

"Thank you," answered Percy, coldly. "I have no wish to learn. A fine sight it would be for you and your friends to see the poor hunchback"—

"Percy, Percy, what do you mean?" cried Hugh, in a tone of horror. "Don't talk like that—please don't."

"Can't you go out of that, Hugh, and leave me alone," shouted Percy. "I'm tired and cold, and you only worry and torment me." And he turned his back on his cousin.

Hugh took his little sister by the hand, and went out into the sunshine, his face flushed and burning, his heart very sad. He longed to make Percy go with him into the park, but he was afraid to say any more, lest he should make matters worse between them.

Mrs. Brown had gone to the kitchen to give orders about the dinner, and was in close confabulation with the cook, when she heard the hall-door shut with a bang. Taking it for granted that the children had all gone off to see the skating, she went up to her own room, where she found many things to occupy her during their absence.

But as the dinner-hour drew near, she went down to the dining-room to see to the arrangement of her table. There, to her surprise, she found Percy alone, sobbing and crying on the sofa.

"Why, my dear Percy, what is the matter?" she asked. "I thought you had gone out hours ago to see the skating. It was very wrong of Hugh to leave you. He" —

"Do not blame Hugh, Aunt Lucy," said Percy, in a sorrowful voice. "He wanted me to go — but I wouldn't, and" —

"He had no right to leave you alone. You, who are always so good — so" —

"Oh, no, I am not good at all," cried the boy. "I made Hugh angry — because — because — it was all my fault — all my wicked temper."

"But, my dear boy, why should you make yourself so unhappy?" said his aunt, sitting down on the couch, and drawing him gently towards her. "You, who have everything you could wish for. You, to whom God has been so good— so" —

"Why do you say that, Aunt Lucy? Why do you say that?" cried Percy, springing to his feet. "How can you look at me and tell me that God has been good to me? How can you think of my misery—my longing for love, that only my darling mother could give to me? For, oh, I am unhappy and miserable—unhappy and miserable;" and flinging himself once more upon the sofa, he sobbed aloud.

"Poor little Percy," said Mrs. Brown, softly, and putting her arm around him she kissed him lovingly. "It is indeed hard to have lost your dear mother; and God has given you many troubles to bear, I know, which would have seemed as nothing had she been spared to you. But just think for a moment of all the blessings he has given you. Think of your good, kind father—how he loves you—how he supplies your every wish. Think of your loving, gentle sister—your happy home—your"—

"But it isn't happy," cried Percy, quickly. "It is wretched and miserable—and, oh, dear, I wish I was dead—I wish I was dead."

"Come, Percy, you must not say that, dear," said his aunt, gently. "You must surely feel that you are not fit to die just now. And only think how terrible it would be, if God were to take you at your word, and hurry you off in your sins. Would it not be dreadful to be cut off—separated from your dear mother forever?"

"Yes, yes; I know it would be terrible. But you see I can't be good. I only grow worse and worse every day. It is so wretched at home—so "—

"Why, Hugh told me you were as happy as possible together. He said you were all so good and kind, and that everything was so pleasant."

"Yes; so it was until Aunt Lydia came and papa went away to the country. She has made me cross and wicked, just when I was getting good. Now I have made Hugh angry, and he will hate me too. I don't know what I shall do. I can't grow good; there's no use trying any more—so I just wish I was dead."

"Our lives are in God's hands, dear lad," said his aunt, gravely. "And it is wrong to wish for death unless in His good time. But now try and cheer up, and do not brood so much over your troubles. Hugh will not be long angry with you, I am sure. My boy would not hate any one for the whole world. He is too anxious to please God to bear malice even to his enemy; and he loves you dearly I know. And as for Mrs. Torrens, I cannot really see how she can make you so unhappy. She is a great lady and fond of company, I hear. But"—

"That is because you don't know her, Aunt Lucy," answered Percy. "She torments me more than any one I ever knew." And then he told her all that happened within the last few weeks.

The kind lady's heart was touched by his story; for, in spite of his many faults, that were only too apparent, she saw much that was good in her poor little nephew. And in his rich home, surrounded by all that wealth could give him, he was unhappy she saw, simply because he would not bear patiently the small trials sent to him by God.

Mrs. Brown was deeply grieved at this, and prayed in her heart that Hugh might be able to understand this strange boy, and help him to conquer his violent temper.

"Well, my dear Percy," she said, after a moment's reflection, "I see that God has sent you many troubles. But what of that? If you bear them patiently, think how great will be your reward. The first thing you must do,

then, is to pray fervently to God. You must
ask him to help you to be gentle and kind."

"But I did—I did. And after Hugh came
I got on so well. Then when Aunt Lydia
appeared I grew worse and"—

" And then you stopped praying and grew
cross and sulky, because something happened
to make your life a little less agreeable."

" But she made my life horrible, and I
couldn't pray any more. It seemed quite useless."

" My dear boy, that is not the right way to
talk of prayer," said his aunt. " The more you
are tempted and tried, the more you must
pray. And, now, I hope you will turn over a
new leaf, and do your best to be polite and
nice to your Aunt Lydia. As far as I can see,
from what you tell me, you have been very
rude to her. Then your conduct last night
was extremely wicked and cowardly. So now,
to show your sorrow for such behavior, you
must bear patiently whatever she may do or
say."

" I will try," sobbed Percy, " I will try."

" And then, consider, dear boy, that although
your troubles seem great to you, they are as
nothing compared with those suffered by Jesus

Christ whilst he was on earth. Think of the patience with which he carried his cross, and yours will seem light indeed. He went all along the road to Calvary, bearing a heavy cross upon his shoulders, without a murmur or complaint. Upon your shoulders he places another cross, which he tells you to carry for his sake. Will you refuse to do so, or carry it, grumbling and complaining as you go?"

"Oh, I will try to carry it bravely! I will, indeed," said Percy. "But you can't think how hard it is."

"Yes, yes; I know it is very hard, dear child; but, then, where would be the merit if it were easy?" and Mrs. Brown laid her hand gently on the golden head. "I know it is hard, Percy, and I feel for you deeply; but there is one thing that will help you greatly, dear, and that is cheerfulness. When you do wrong, do not fret and chafe about it, or try to put the blame on any one else. Turn to God, tell him you are sorry, and then be as bright as possible; for in giving way to gloom and despair, you may offend your heavenly Father still more."

"But that is just what I can't do. I can't be cheerful," cried Percy. "When I do wrong,

I feel sorry—at least, angry at myself for having done it. Then I get sulky and ill-tempered; so that I go on getting worse and worse; and then I'm wretched and miserable."

"Of course, you are, dear child; but if you will just bear each little trouble, as it comes, for God, you will soon find how much lighter it will grow. Try to be bright, good-tempered, and patient, and all will be well. Be respectful to your Aunt Lydia when you see her, and I am sure she will be kind to you."

"I will do the best I can," said Percy, "and I will try hard to pray. Will you let me come to see you often, Aunt Lucy, and let me talk to you about myself?"

"Certainly, dear. Come as often as you can," said his aunt kindly. "You are my darling sister's child, and it will be a great happiness for me if I can help you a little. But, indeed, Percy dear, if you knew the troubles some people have to bear, you would not think much of your own."

"I wouldn't mind anything half so much, aunt," said Percy, flushing painfully, "if—if my back was straight like other boys; but people hate hunchbacks—and—and that will always keep me unhappy."

"My dear, dear lad," cried Mrs. Brown, greatly distressed at this speech, "that is a cruel thought and a false one, I am sure. Why should any one hate you because of that? You are as God made you, and he has good reasons for all he does. Whoever told you that was cruelly wicked and wrong. Be good and gentle and every one will love you, every one will respect you, no matter how you are made."

"Ah, yes, if I were good," said Percy, sadly; "but it seems to me, aunt, that ever since my mother's death I have been under a cloud, which year after year grows heavier and heavier, making life harder to bear every day that I live."

"That is, very likely, quite true, dear boy. But I am afraid it is because you have not taken the right way to free yourself from that cloud. You have always wanted to have your own way in everything, and have not tried to bear your troubles with patience."

"I find it so hard to be patient," said Percy, sighing. "But I will begin to try very hard from to-day."

"That is right," she answered, with a kiss. "Where there is a will there's a way. But don't expect to grow patient all at once, dear

boy. That would be impossible. It takes
us many years to conquer one small fault,
thoroughly. But if we struggle hard, and
pray fervently, God will help us, and then all
will go right. But run upstairs and make
yourself fresh and tidy. Here comes Mary to
lay the cloth; and, I declare, Hugh and Susie
are coming in at the gate."

As they all sat round the table at dinner,
little Susie was very lively, and chattered away
at a wonderful rate.

The ice had been so thick and strong; the
ladies so bright and beautiful; everything in
the Park enchanting. Then, Hugh whirled her
along so fast; they had seen so many "jolly
falls"; and Susie's sweet laugh rang out merrily through the room, as she told them of all
these delightful things.

She looked at Hugh, and he laughed gayly
at her stories. She looked at Percy and her
mother, but they seemed so serious that the
child wondered greatly.

"Oh, why," she thought, "are they so sad
when everything is so gay and pleasant?"
Then, remembering some funny incident that
had occurred upon the ice, Susie burst into a
fresh peal of laughter.

Such childish gayety is very contagious, and, at last, even Percy joined in the fun. Greatly amused by one of the little girl's quaint speeches, he smiled upon her, and began to talk. And so, for the present, the clouds were cleared away.

And when dinner was over, Percy slipped his hand into Hugh's, and asked him to forgive him for his cross, ill-natured words.

"Of course I do, old chap," was Hugh's reply. "I am really sorry that I went to the Park without you; for it was jolly there."

"I don't mind about that; but I am going to be so good, Hugh. And mind, you must help me."

"To be sure I will. Come now and have a game of blind-man's-buff with Susie." But as the short winter's day drew to a close, and the ponies were heard jingling their bells at the gate, the romps were brought to a speedy conclusion, and the boys had to get ready for their drive.

Poor Susie's face clouded, and her blue eyes filled with tears, as she hung around Hugh, begging him not to go away, but just to stay, and live with them at the cottage.

"My darling wee sister," said Hugh, with a

loving kiss, "I couldn't do that. But we shall come another day soon. Eh, Percy?"

"Yes, indeed, we will; that is, if Aunt Lucy will have us."

"My dear boy, you will always be most welcome," said Mrs. Brown, smiling. "Will you come on Saturday and bring Theo with you?"

"That will be delightful," cried Percy. "Thank you, so much, dear aunt."

"Well, good-by till then, mother," said Hugh, with a hug. "Take care of yourself and my darling Susie."

"I am quite sure to do that, dear child," she said, pressing him to her heart. "Good-by, and God bless you, my brave, true son."

Then the boys kissed tiny Susie over and over again, and promised to bring all kinds of good things with them on Saturday. This comforted the little girl, and drying her tears she smiled and kissed her hand gayly, as she stood watching them get into the phaeton.

"Our Hoo's a dood, dood boy, muver," she said, as her mother tucked her up in bed for the night.

"A good lad, indeed, Susie," answered Mrs. Brown, earnestly. "But we must ask God to keep him good always, dear. He will have many trials and temptations, as he goes through life."

"But, muver, dear, God is sure to take care of him; for every morning I say, 'God bless Hoo, and make him a dood boy, and don't let any harm come to him.' And you know God is sure to do what we ask him."

And having uttered this act of faith in the goodness of God, Susie kissed her mother, and fell asleep.

CHAPTER XI.

BURGLARS IN THE HOUSE.

"HUGH," said Percy, as they drove along, "I have been having a talk with Aunt Lucy, and she has given me some very good advice."

"Dear old mother! Doesn't she talk beautifully?" cried Hugh, his eyes shining with love.

"Yes, indeed, she does. And I tell you what, Hugh, I have been thinking over all she said to me about being civil to Aunt Lydia. So I am sure the best thing for me to do, is to go straight up to her room and beg her pardon for the way I frightened her last night."

"I think it would certainly be a good thing. But do you feel as if you could do it properly?" asked Hugh, doubtfully; for he could not imagine that the boy's passionate nature would allow him to beg his aunt's pardon in a sufficiently humble manner. "You see she will be very angry, old fellow, and"—

"Yes, yes, I know. But I feel, some way, as if it would be easier to be polite after I had begged her pardon. She can't help forgiving me when I tell her how sorry I am."

"No; I think not; but—why I declare, there is the carriage at the door," cried Hugh, as they turned into Holland Park. "You can just speak to her in the hall for a minute. I suppose she is off to a dinner party."

"So it would seem," said Percy, his heart sinking within him, as he thought of the disagreeable task he had to perform. "Keep as close to me as possible, Hugh," he whispered, as he jumped out of the phaeton. "I feel horribly nervous, and would love to run away."

The groom drove off with the ponies, and the two boys walked slowly into the hall.

The butler and footmen were all there, waiting about till Mrs. Torrens should descend from her room, and go forth in state, to keep one of her many dinner engagements.

"Don't speak to her now, Percy. Wait till to-morrow morning to beg her pardon," whispered Hugh. "I don't like you to do it before the servants. Wait till to-morrow and you can do it quietly in the dining-room."

"But, my dear Hugh, I must. I feel as if it must be done now, or never," he answered. "The men won't mind; they shan't hear what I am saying, and, if they do, what matter?"

Just as he spoke the rustle of silken garments was heard, and Mrs. Torrens, in rich evening dress, swept down the stairs into the hall, Theo running gayly behind, carrying her fan, lace handkerchief, and scent bottle.

As she turned to take these things from the little girl, the lady's face looked kind and pleasant; but when her eyes fell upon Percy and his cousin, an angry flush rose to her brow, the smile faded from her lips, and with a glance of hatred, she gathered up her trailing skirts and walked quickly past them.

But Percy was so anxious to carry out his good resolutions, so occupied with the thought of begging her pardon, that he did not notice her angry looks. So, instead of taking Hugh's advice and waiting till the next morning, he dashed forward, and in the presence of the servants, whispered that he was sorry, very sorry, for his conduct of the night before. At the sound of his voice, Mrs. Torrens turned, and without the slightest pity for the boy, burst forth angrily :

"How dare you speak to me? How dare you come near me? You cruel, bad boy. You should be horse-whipped well for your conduct last night."

"Indeed, Aunt Lydia "—

"Do not call me Aunt Lydia, please. You would kill me if you could, I am sure ; for, like all other hunchbacks, you are bad-hearted and cruel "—

"No, indeed, I did not wish to kill you," cried Percy, his eyes beginning to blaze. "I only wanted to frighten you, and make you think the house was haunted, and "—

"And then you thought I would run away, I suppose," she said, with a scornful laugh. "But I will do no such thing; and if you try it again I'll find some way to punish you. But don't talk to me of forgiveness, you wicked "—

"Do not be so hard, Mrs. Torrens," cried Hugh, coming forward and putting his arm round Percy, as though to protect him from her fury.

"Hard, indeed," she cried, glaring at him fiercely. "Who are you, pray, that you should dare to preach to me? The son of an adventuress who has managed to pass herself off on my brother as his wife's sister. A little street boy brought in to teach these foolish children all kinds of wicked tricks, and "—

"Indeed, you wrong me, Mrs. Torrens," cried Hugh; "I am Sir Henry's nephew, and I never "—

"Do not interrupt me, sir. How dare you deny it? Right well I know it was you who made this boy turn upon me as he did last night. It was you put it into his head to frighten me out of the house. It was you who carried him off to-day, that he might show the disrespect he feels for me, that he might escape the just punishment I had in store for him. So now you may go, I have found you out. My brother is absent, and I am mistress here. Leave the house this instant. I will not allow you two to pass another night together, to plot and plan any further mischief. Sir Henry shall hear of your conduct, and whether you are his nephew or not he will surely approve of what I have done. Away you go this minute; I will not stir from this till I see you out. I am in a hurry, so I beg that you will not keep me waiting," and she tapped her foot impatiently on the floor.

"He shall not go," cried Percy, starting forward, his cheeks flaming, his whole body quivering with passion. "You have no right to send my cousin away. I am master in my father's house, and he shall not go."

"But he shall and must," replied Mrs. Torrens, pointing imperiously to the door. "If he does not go at once, I will call a policeman and hand him over to him, and then "—

"Good-night, Percy dear, and don't fret about me. It is best for me to go," whispered Hugh. "When my uncle comes home you can tell him all about it, and send for me to come back," and, wringing his cousin's hand, the boy took up his hat, rushed out of the house, and away down the dark road that led to Richmond.

"The carriage," called Mrs. Torrens, in an awful voice, as Hugh disappeared. Then, gathering her silken skirts once more around her, she swept down the steps, without a word of comfort to the unhappy Percy, who stood pale and silent, gazing out into the night, apparently unconscious of all that was going on about him.

"Percy dear, I am so sorry," whispered Theo, as the door was closed, and the servants had withdrawn to the lower regions, to talk and wonder over this strange affair. "Hugh will soon come back, never fear. Papa won't believe that he's wicked, I know quite well," and the girl's arms were thrown lovingly round her brother's neck.

"Leave me alone," muttered Percy, shaking her off roughly. "I want none of your pity. How I hate you, Aunt Lydia—oh, how I hate you," he cried, grinding his teeth, and shaking his fist at the spot where Mrs. Torrens had stood last. "I hate you, although you are my father's sister, for you make me feel so wicked and horrible, just when"—

Then, covering his face with his hands, he rushed down the passage to his room, where he flung himself on the floor in an agony of grief.

Theo's kind little heart was filled with compassion, and she would gladly have comforted the unhappy boy if she could; but when she heard him lock his door, she knew he would not speak to her again that night. She was frightened at his words of passion and hatred, and wept bitterly as she sat alone on the stairs.

At last a bright idea seemed to strike her; for, drying her eyes, she went quickly upstairs to the school-room. Taking out her little desk, she sat down by the fire and wrote a few lines to her father, imploring him to come home, as they were all very miserable without him.

When this was done, Theo felt somewhat happier, and went off to bed, fondly hoping that everything would come right next morning.

At half-past eleven, the carriage came driving up to the door, bearing Mrs. Torrens home from her dinner-party. Just as the footman announced the lady's arrival by a violent peal at the bell, a gentleman jumped out of a "hansom," and Sir Henry Randall came forward to greet his sister.

"Dear, dear, how you startled me," she exclaimed. "I thought you were miles away. What on earth brought you home in such a hurry?"

"A longing to see the bairns," he said, laughingly, as he helped her to alight. "I felt a great desire to see their bonnie faces once more. I came up by the mail; but, as it was late, I dined at the club. The chicks will get a joyful surprise when I walk in to breakfast in the morning. I hope they are all quite well?"

" Yes, they are well," she answered grimly. " But you can judge for yourself when you see them. It is too late for any further conversation. I am tired, so I will say good-night."

And she went away to her room, leaving Sir Henry standing alone in the hall.

" It is strange how little she cares for those poor children," he murmured, as he looked after her with a sad expression on his kindly face. " And yet how happy she might make them if — but why should I think of such a thing when they never could agree. Poor Percy — poor lad — how your mother loved and cherished you. How different your life was while she was near you. I wonder what they have all been about during my absence. I wish I had come a little sooner and seen them before they went to bed, for I feel as if something must be wrong — Lydia looked so stern and angry. But I must wait till the morning for news. It is very late, so they are sure to be all asleep. Turn out the gas, Grey, and bolt the door," he said to the butler, who stood waiting for orders. "I want nothing more to-night."

And then Sir Henry passed up the stairs, walking very softly, lest he should wake the sleeping children.

The great clock in the hall stuck one; the whole house was dark and silent, and yet Sir Henry could not settle to rest. A vague feeling of alarm was upon him; and in spite of the fatigue he felt, after his long journey from Scotland, he could not bring himself to go to bed, but paced his room from end to end, trying in vain to shake off the anxious thoughts that kept crowding in upon him.

At last he determined that, late as it was, he would see Percy, and make sure that all was well with him. So, taking up a candle, he opened his door and passed out on to the landing.

But as he went he thought how foolish he was; how unkind it would be to wake the child for nothing, and he was about to return to his room when an agonizing cry sounded through the house.

"What is that? What is that? What can have happened?" cried Sir Henry.

But as he spoke Percy came running along

the hall below. A cloak was thrown over his night-shirt, his hair was wild and tumbled, and he had neither shoes nor stockings on his feet.

"Robbers! burglars! thieves!" he screamed with all his strength. "Help — help. Oh, come and help me — come and help me!"

At this sudden realization of his worst fears, Sir Henry dropped his candle, and springing down the dark staircase, caught the boy in his arms.

Believing his father to be far away in Scotland, and not recognizing him in the obscure light, Percy uttered a wild prayer for mercy, and would have fallen fainting to the ground, had it not been for the strong arm that was round him.

Sir Henry raised the unconscious boy, and bore him swiftly up the stairs to his own room. Laying him gently on the bed he called for Bridget, the children's old nurse, to come and attend him as fast as she could. Then, without waiting for his son to recover his senses, he hurried away to see what had caused him such serious alarm.

"What is the matter, Henry? What can be the matter?" screamed Mrs. Torrens, in a terrified voice, as he passed her door.

" Nothing that need alarm you, Lydia. Go back to your bed. There is no fear of the burglars coming up here now," he answered; then ran on quickly to the hall.

" Nothing to alarm me, indeed," she cried, indignantly, " and you going shrieking and shouting about the house in the middle of the night. But, if there are burglars down there, I shall take pretty good care they don't come near me." And she withdrew to her chamber, locking and bolting the door behind her.

Meanwhile, Sir Henry, Grey, and the two footmen entered Percy's room cautiously and silently. They peered about into every corner; shook every curtain, and opened every door. But not a creature could be found; and they at last concluded that the robbers had escaped when Percy had given the alarm to the household.

But everything within the room was in a state of wild confusion. Silver forks and spoons lay in heaps upon the table and floor; the precious treasures from the much-loved cabinet were thrown here and there about the place, and just outside the open window lay a beautiful silver tea-pot, which they had probably tried to carry off, but had dropped accidentally in their flight.

And when Sir Henry approached the little alcove in which his son slept, he started back with an exclamation of horror.

Sticking up out of the mattress was a huge carving-knife, which must have been aimed at the boy in hopes of killing him as he slept.

"Those rascals must be found," he cried. "Call in the watchman, that I may give him the particulars of this murderous attack on my son's life. It will, indeed, be a terrible thing if we cannot trace these wicked wretches."

The policeman came and listened gravely to the story. He advised them to search the lower part of the premises, and if no one was seen, to fasten up the doors and windows and go to bed.

They did as he desired, but no further traces of the burglars could be found. So the man bade Sir Henry a respectful good-night, and took his departure, promising to keep a sharp look-out upon the house for the remainder of the night.

The servants then set to work to put their young master's room in order again.

They carried the spoons and forks back to

the safe in the library, and were much surprised to find that this had not been broken open, as they had supposed, but had been unlocked with the key in the proper manner.

"Grey," said the master, in a stern voice, "this key was in your charge during my absence. How does it come that you left it about for burglars to make use of?"

"I beg your pardon, Sir Henry, but I did not leave it about," said Grey, respectfully. "I locked up the silver, and placed the key in the drawer in your bedroom, as I always do, at half past nine this evening."

"Then I cannot understand how the thieves can have found it. That drawer is hard to open unless one knows the secret. But we shall know more to-morrow. Go up, Thomas, and see how Master Percy is. I think I will not go near him again, lest I should startle him. I will stay in his room for to-night.

The man went away, and returned in a few minutes, saying that Percy was restless, and called continually for his cousin.

"Poor lad, poor lad," said his father, "this has been a great shock for him. Ask Master Hugh to go to him. I wonder he has not been down all this time. But boys do sleep so soundly. I dare say he has not heard the slightest noise. You might knock at his door, Thomas, and tell him that Master Percy is not well. He will go to him immediately, I am sure."

"But—if—you please, Sir 'Enery," began Thomas.

"Well, what is the matter? Are you afraid to go up stairs again alone?"

"No, Sir 'Enery; but Master 'Ugh, Sir 'Enery"—

"Well, what about Master Hugh? You are not afraid to wake him, I suppose. It is a pity, poor boy, but it can't be helped."

"I don't mind wakin' 'im, Sir 'Enery. But please—'es gone. 'Es not in 'is room."

"Hugh not in his room? Hugh gone!" cried his master in astonishment. "Where has he gone? When did he go?"

"If you please, Sir Henry," said Grey, bowing respectfully, "Master Hugh Brown left the house this evening at a quarter to eight, by orders of your sister, Mrs. Torrens."

CHAPTER XII.

A STRANGE CONFESSION.

THE next morning Percy looked pale and weary. He did not go downstairs to breakfast, but took it alone in the old nursery, which had long since become the special sanctum of Nurse Bridget. This good woman loved the boy dearly, and was sorely vexed to see him so ill. But she put it down to the fright he had received the night before, and talked to him about all manner of pleasant things, hoping to cheer him up, and make him forget the terrible midnight visitors.

But no matter what she did or said, Percy remained sad and preoccupied; and at last Bridget turned away with a sigh, and taking her knitting, sat down in silence by the fire.

"Nurse," said Percy, a few moments later, "I want to ask you something."

"Ask away, my son, I'll gladly tell you all I know," she answered, smiling.

"Why—why—did that robber put me into papa's bed?"

"That robber—that— Dear, bless my soul, Master Percy, I don't believe the robbers came up the stairs at all. Leastways they were very quiet if they did. But it seems more likely to me that Mr. Grey left the key of the safe ready waitin' in the lock. But, of course, it's not for me to say. But, dear heart alive, it was your own dear father caught you in his arms as you were just goin' to fall senseless on"—

"Was it really my father—really?"

"Yes; really and truly your own dear father that carried you up and laid you on his own bed."

"But I thought papa was in Scotland—I thought—oh, dear, how shall I tell him? How shall I ever look him in the face? If I had only known he was at home," and, to Bridget's surprise, Percy began to cry.

"Poor lad, poor lad," she said kindly, and, putting her arm around him, she led him to the sofa and tried to make him lie down and rest.

But Percy started away from her, and flinging himself on a chair declared that he should never be able to speak to his father again; that he would run away; that he would die; and made so many wild statements of this kind that poor old nurse thought he must be going quite mad.

"Dear, dear, I must go for Sir Henry—I must, indeed," she cried, going to the door.

"Nurse, nurse," called Percy, and she was beside him in an instant.

"Tell me truly. Was it really my father who caught me in his arms last night?"

"Yes, it was indeed. But, if you do not believe me, go down and ask Sir Henry. He will tell you all about it."

"No, no; I can't do that," cried Percy, and he covered his face with his hands.

As he now seemed to have grown somewhat calmer, Bridget took up her knitting and sat down, hoping every moment that he would think better of what he had said and go down stairs to his father.

But Percy remained where he was with a weary look about him as though too tired to speak or move. The least sound in the passage or on the stairs made him flush violently,

and he trembled visibly when a door opened
or shut.

But, at last, a servant came with a message
from Sir Henry, saying that he would be glad
to see his son in the library as soon as possible.

"Tell him I can't go. Tell him I—at
least—no—I will go directly," Percy said
nervously; then sank back upon his chair,
looking white and frightened.

"Oh, I suppose I must go; I suppose I
must; I am longing to see him and yet I
dread to meet him. Never in my life did I feel
so ashamed to; but I must—I must;" and,
springing suddenly to his feet, he dashed out
of the room and down the stairs.

Terrified by this unexpected display of
strength, Bridget ran after him along the passage; she was afraid he might fall fainting
once more, if there was no one near to help
him on his way.

But Percy was not so weak as he appeared,
and very soon vanished from her sight. Then,
presently she heard the library door open and
shut; and, with a sigh of relief, she returned
to her own quarters.

When Percy entered the room Sir Henry
was standing by the fire, talking to Theo,

whose face was radiant with joy at feeling her dear father's arm around her once more.

" You must not go away without me again, dear papa," she said, rubbing her cheek against his hand. " I have been so miserable whilst you were away, and I was terrified when I heard about the robbers last night. Why, if you had not come home in time, they might have killed us all ; and, as for poor Percy he — But here he comes to speak for himself at last," and she sprang forward to kiss her brother.

" Percy ! Percy ! here is papa," she cried. " Is it not glorious to have him home again ? Didn't those burglars give you a fright, poor boy; and isn't it lucky they didn't kill you with that big knife ? "

" My dear Theo, what a stream of questions. How can you expect any one to answer you, if you ask so many things at once ? " said Sir Henry, laughing. " But why are you so pale, Percy, dear lad ? " and, taking his little son in his arms, he kissed him tenderly.

" I don't feel very well, papa," replied Percy, flushing.

" You are nervous, dear, after the shock you received last night, and no wonder. But, cheer up, my boy ; we shall soon discover those rascals of robbers, and I shall make an example of them, I promise you. And now, I want you to tell me all you can — what you saw; what the men were like; and so on."

"No, no; please no, papa; don't ask me; I would rather not; I — there — was — nothing taken — and " —

"Nothing taken? How can you be sure of that yet? All the forks and spoons that were over your room show very clearly that the fellows knew what they were about. I am pretty certain they took a great many things away with them. Why, we even found a tea-pot on the garden-wall. Whoever took that, took more, you may be quite sure. I will ask Grey if he has gone over the silver. We shall then have an idea of how much has been stolen."

The bell was rung, and the butler appeared; but he declared that, having counted the silver, as Sir Henry had desired, he found that there was not so much as a teaspoon missing.

"Now, father, aren't you quite satisfied," cried Percy, eagerly. Let the men alone, you " —

"Indeed, I am not at all satisfied, Percy," replied his father, hotly. "There must be some way of tracing those ruffians who have entered my house and attempted my son's life; for, had you not escaped — as you told Bridget last night, by slipping down between the bed and the wall — you would surely have been killed by that knife, which I found sticking in your mattress!"

"Yes, I know; but how are you to trace these robbers, papa?" said Percy, nervously. "The light was so dim, that I should never know the men again; and then — and then — you might blame some innocent person."

"There is no fear of that," cried a voice that made Percy start and flush; "I can give you something to help you to find the thieves; I can give you a clue — put you on the right track," and, and with a look of triumph, Mrs. Torrens flung two empty jewel cases upon the table. "What do you say to that, Henry? My diamond star and bracelet were stolen from these last night; and I believe, and solemnly declare, that Hugh Brown headed the band of robbers that entered the house, and showed them" —

"That is a lie, and you know it is," cried Percy, passionately.

"For shame, Percy," cried his father.

"You hear him, brother. I am very glad,"

said Mrs. Torrens. "Now, perhaps, you will understand the contemptuous manner in which your son always treats me. But we shall say no more upon the subject for the present. I must now set to work to find my jewels, and I shall feel much obliged if you will kindly assist me as far as you can. It will be a difficult task, no doubt, but if you will help me, I shall soon get them back, I am sure."

"Of course I will do all I possibly can to assist you, Lydia," Sir Henry replied; "but I am deeply pained that you should bring such an accusation against Hugh. It was cruel of you to do so, and I sincerely hope that you will recall your words when you have time for reflection."

"I am quite sure I shall do no such thing," she answered, haughtily. "I have good reason to think that I am right, and am certain to hear nothing to induce me to change."

"But, my dear Lydia, the idea is most preposterous. Hugh is my nephew, and a better or more honest lad I never knew in my life."

"Yes; and you know him for such a long time. My dear Henry, even supposing the boy were really your nephew, which I don't believe, what do you know about him?

Brought up, as he has been, in the backwoods of Australia, and then in a wretched lodging in London, is it likely that he is the paragon you wish to make him out? I, for one, never had any faith in the youngster, and am not at all astonished at what has happened. Some one in the house helped those men last night."

"But Hugh was not in the house, aunt," cried Theo; "you sent him away."

"Of course, I know that, Miss Pert," replied Mrs. Torrens; "but what I mean is, that some one who knew the house and its ways helped the burglars; some one who knew where my room was, and where my jewels were kept; some one who knew where the key of the plate-chest was to be found; and that some one was no other than Hugh Brown, in spite of his meek looks and quiet ways. I saw mischief in his face as he left the hall yesterday evening. He hated me, and, when I turned him out last night, I felt sure that he would be revenged upon me as soon as he could."

"And why you treated the boy so shamefully I cannot understand," said Sir Henry. "Had I been at home I would not have allowed you to do so."

"Had you heard my reason for turning him

out, perhaps you would not defend him so warmly," she cried.

"I have heard the reason, and I cannot see any justice in it," answered her brother, warmly. "Percy played a wicked trick upon you, and you wreak your anger on Hugh, who had no more to do with it than he has had to do with the stealing of your diamonds last night."

"Indeed, so you think!" she said, scornfully.

"So I believe confidently," he replied. "I am certain that Hugh had as little to do with it as Percy or I."

"Far less, far less," cried Percy, twisting his fingers nervously together; "far less, for he was away in Richmond."

"Yes, I am sure he went home to his mother," said Sir Henry. "I will go there after lunch, Lydia, and question him closely. It will not be difficult to learn the truth from his frank, open countenance."

"Question him, indeed," cried Mrs. Torrens, fiercely. "I shall send a policeman to arrest him, and then we shall hear him questioned before a magistrate," and gathering up her jewel cases she turned to leave the room.

But Percy darted forward, and clutching convulsively at her dress, implored her to stay where she was for a few moments longer.

"I have something to tell you about last night, Aunt Lydia," he said, in a hoarse whisper. "Pray listen to what I have to tell you."

"Bah, what can you have to tell me?" she replied, angrily, and trying to shake him off. "I know all you have to tell me. I have heard your story over and over again from Mary Ann. How you saw three great black-looking men poking about your room; how one came and glared at you in your bed, and how you saved yourself by slipping underneath. Oh, I know it all; but what do I care? I want my diamonds—my"—

"Yes, yes, I know," cried Percy, with quivering lip. "But I want to tell you—to swear to you that Hugh was not here last night."

"Nonsense, boy! Let me go. Why on earth should you make such a fuss, because I have proof that that wretched little adventurer is a thief. It is only what you might all have expected."

"But listen—pray listen," insisted Percy. "Father, do make her stay. She must not arrest Hugh. She must not accuse him falsely, my dear, good cousin. Speak to her, father; beg her not to be so hard—not to go till she hears what I have to tell—till "—

"She shall not, my dear boy," cried Sir Henry, stroking the golden hair. "Lydia, I must ask you to sit down for a few minutes, as a personal favor. That is right. Now, Percy, do not keep your aunt too long. Calm yourself, and tell us quietly what you want to say."

As Mrs. Torrens could not well refuse her brother's request, she flung herself down upon the sofa with an angry glare at Percy.

"Be quick with your story, please. My time is precious," she said, ungraciously; "and I do not care to waste it listening to your nonsense."

"What I have to say must be said before the servants, papa," said Percy, growing white to the lips. "Will you ring, and ask them all to come up?"

"Mighty theatrical, upon my word," sneered Mrs. Torrens.

"My dear child," cried his father, in surprise, "what can the servants have to do with it? You are too much agitated; you are ill. Come and lie down. You can tell us this secret later on.   Your aunt will listen to you this evening, I am sure."

"For Hugh's sake it must be done at once," answered Percy, with a gasp.   "Don't touch me, father; don't look at me kindly till you have heard my story—and—and forgiven me. But please do as I ask you.   Ring the bell and ask the servants to come up."

Seeing that the boy was really in earnest, Sir Henry rang the bell and requested the butler to collect the servants and bring them to speak to him in the library.

Greatly alarmed at such an unexpected summons the numerous domestics came hurrying in, and ranged themselves in silence along the furthest end of the room.

"Now, Percy, my lad, let us hear this wonderful tale of yours," cried Sir Henry, as cheerfully as possible; for he wished to help the child, whose extreme agitation gave him great anxiety.

Percy stood by the table, pale as death; and as his father spoke he grasped the back of a chair, as though to steady himself, ere he began.   He trembled so much that little Theo thought he must surely fall, and she whispered to him to sit down and rest for a moment.

But Percy did not hear her, and casting his eyes upon the ground, he said, faintly:

" Father, there were no robbers in the house last night."

" No robbers? My dear boy, you are — you must be dreaming."

" No, father, I am not dreaming," said Percy, his voice growing stronger as he spoke. " What I say is true. There were no burglars in the house nor in my room. I threw open the window; I threw the silver about the floor and then ran out shouting for help as I " —

" Percy, why did you do such a monstrous thing?" cried Sir Henry. " What could have possessed you to act such a lie? I really cannot believe it possible."

" But you must believe me, father. I did it because I wanted to be revenged — because I wanted to frighten Aunt Lydia, and make her leave the house. I " —

" A very creditable confession, upon my word," exclaimed Mrs. Torrens, indignantly; " and now, perhaps you will tell me where my jewels are; and how you managed to enter my room unseen last night after I was in bed. I wore the star and bracelet at the dinner party, so " —

"About your jewels I know nothing," answered Percy, quickly. "I did not touch a single thing except the silver, and I never went near your room. I did not go up stairs till I ran up shouting for help. Then my father caught me in his arms and carried me to his bedroom. I was terrified when I saw him, for I did not recognize him, and thought some burglars had really got in — that he was one and would kill me — and " —

"You tell a story well, my charming nephew," said Mrs. Torrens, with a scornful laugh. "But I tell you plainly that I do not believe one word of it. The whole thing is a make-up — a wicked lie, told to screen that young adventurer whom you call your cousin, Hugh Brown."

" Indeed — indeed, it is every word true. Hugh was not here — Hugh " —

" I would not believe a word you say, Percy Randall," she answered, contemptuously, " not if you were to swear it."

" But I tell you it is true, and you must believe me," cried Percy, passionately. " Father, tell her it is true. Ask her to believe me and spare Hugh," and he turned imploringly to Sir Henry who stood stern and silent by the fire.

"I cannot believe you, either, Percy." he replied, in a tone of deep pain. "A boy who could act as you have done, would be so mean, so wretched, that I could not bear to think of him as my son. You have told a story that is to me perfectly incredible. If you have played this trick, you have acted a series of lies, of which I could never believe you capable. And if you have told this tale hoping to screen Hugh, say so; and although I shall feel grieved beyond measure to think that you could tell such a lie, still, as it has been told in a good cause, with a kind intention, I may forgive you in time. But if this account of last night's work be true — if you have acted the coward's part that you describe" —

"Father — father — I did — I did; but forgive me — forgive me," cried Percy, wildly; and he flung himself at Sir Henry's feet.

"I cannot forgive you," said his father, sternly, and he turned away from the kneeling boy. "You have acted as only a wicked, revengeful creature could do. I am ashamed of you, and cannot bear to think that my son ceuld be guilty of such conduct. Go — retire to your room, and, think over your wickedness in silence and alone. I will not hear another word from you at present. Go."

Never before had Percy heard his father's voice so hard and stern; never before had he spoken to him in such a determined manner.

So, without daring to utter another prayer for pardon, without a murmur at his harshness, he rose to his feet and crept out of the library.

Almost blind with terror, he groped his way along the passage to his room, there to weep bitter tears of mingled grief and rage over his miserable conduct and cruel treatment.

CHAPTER XIII.

PERCY GIVES WAY TO DESPAIR.

THE time dragged wearily on, and Percy remained alone in his room, miserable and unhappy.

The house was strangely silent all through the day, and as evening closed in, the boy began to long for the sight of a friendly face.

His door had been locked since morning, and no one had sought leave to enter except the servant, whom his father had sent with his luncheon. But Percy was too wretched to think of eating, and took no notice of the man's knock for admission.

"Poor little genelman, 'e'll come out maybe, and take it in if I just leave it 'ere," said Thomas to himself, and depositing the tray on a table near the door, he went away.

And as time passed over and no one came to

comfort him, Percy became more and more unhappy.

He had wept so long and bitterly that his eyes were swelled and burning, his lips hot, his throat dry and parched.

"Oh, father, father, if you could only forgive me," he cried, raising his aching head for a moment, then letting it fall again upon his out-stretched arms. "Forgive me, father—forgive your poor little son."

But his father could not hear his prayer, and did not understand the depth of the boy's misery. He had not shown much sorrow when telling his story in the library, and was boldly defiant in his manner, so Sir Henry thought it best to leave him alone, hoping that a few hours' solitude would bring him to a proper state of good feeling and subjection.

And thus it was that the poor boy was deserted at a time when a loving word might have touched and softened his heart.

Had his mother been alive she would have understood this well, and would have saved her child from the sad consequences of this day of loneliness and neglect.

But, alas, she was not near, and Percy was left alone, with no companions but his own proud, angry thoughts, which he had never been taught to curb or subdue.

Over and over again he went through the scene in the library, and each time it seemed more and more impossible that he should ever obtain his father's forgiveness.

"And yet I felt sure he would forgive me at once when he saw how much it pained me to tell it to them all," he said, bitterly. "But, oh, how cruel he was. How hard and stern. And only for Hugh — for the love I have for him — I would never have told. I never meant to tell; and if papa had just remained a little longer in Scotland, it would all have gone off quietly enough. Aunt Lydia would have been frightened, no robbers would have been found, and that would have been the end of it. But then when he came home, and the diamonds were lost and Hugh accused, I had to tell. Oh, dear, oh, dear, what an unfortunate boy I am. How delighted Aunt Lydia was to see me scorned before the servants; how happy it made her to see me sent away in disgrace."

And at this thought Percy writhed with pain. He stamped his feet and gnashed his teeth as he remembered his aunt's delight at his cruel humiliation.

"I can't bear to think of it," he cried, fiercely. "I have been shamefully treated by every one, and it is too bad. Papa should not have said such things before Aunt Lydia; if he had told me quietly that it was wicked I shouldn't have minded — but to be scorned and —. But I can't stand it, and I won't. Perhaps he may want me to beg her pardon, and before the servants too. But I won't — so there. Aunt Lucy is good and kind — Aunt Lucy will not treat me as papa has treated me, so I shall go to her and tell her all about it. If my father wants me back again he can come for me."

This seemed a delightful way of escaping from further humiliation for the present at least, and Percy grasped at it at once. So, starting to his feet, he seized his hat and coat, and began to put them on with great alacrity.

"But supposing my father should never forgive me? Supposing he should never let me come home again? Supposing he were to send me away to a horrid school — to — to punish me? What should I do? How could I live away from my home — away from" — and he glanced round the room, gazing at all his treasures with looks of loving regret.

"But no, that is impossible. My father loves me too well for that; he will soon send for me. He will be frightened when he finds me gone. Then he will come to look for me; will see how cruel he has been; and will forgive me at once. Aunt Lydia will go away, I will come back, and we shall be happy again together. But I could not bear to see my father to-night, or even to-morrow—I could not bear to hear him speak to me in that stern voice again. He does not love me—at least not to-day—so I'll just go off to Aunt Lucy and Hugh. They will never turn against me."

So, allowing himself to be blinded by pride, Percy misjudged his loving father, and revolted against his well-deserved punishment.

And yet, here, had he but thought of it, was an excellent opportunity of putting in practice the good resolutions he had made, and profiting by the advice he had received from Mrs. Brown only the day before.

But, alas! all that was now forgotten; he thought no more of being patient and virtuous; he neglected to pray to his Heavenly Father for help in this hour of temptation; and in trying to escape from suffering and humiliation, he fell into a more terrible danger.

Without giving himself time for further reflection, the foolish boy resolved to leave the house and set out for Richmond at once. So, snatching up a warm muffler, he tied it tightly round his throat, pulled his hat over his brows, and passed quickly down the long passage into the hall.

Here he paused for an instant and listened cautiously, lest any of the household should be about and see him go out.

But no one was near, and he sped silently past the library door, up the wide hall, and out into the street.

It was now quite dark; and as the keen evening air chilled him to the heart, he began to realize what a foolish thing he was doing; and, gulping down a big sob that rose in his throat, he turned as though to enter the house again.

But the door had closed behind him, and in order to regain his room it would be necessary to ring the bell and summon the servants; then his folly would be made known in an instant, and lead to further trouble.

" It must be done now," he murmured sadly. " I dare not return, so I must hurry on to Richmond. Even if the cold were to kill me,

I would not let Thomas see me, or guess what I had wanted to do and couldn't."

So, buttoning his coat up tightly round his throat, he dashed quickly along, intending to take a cab whenever he found himself at some distance from Holland Park.

Percy's ideas of money and its value were rather vague, and he imagined that a few pounds would be sufficient to keep him from want for a very long time.

But, although he had not considered the question of ways and means very deeply, still he did know that in order to take a cab it was necessary to have ready money with which to pay his fare when he reached his destination. So all at once he began to wonder how much he really had in his possession.

His father had always kept him well supplied with pocket-money, and his purse was generally pretty full. He remembered that only a few days before, he had given him a five-pound note, with which to buy a mechanical engine that he had seen and admired.

" I shall not want that engine now," he said with a groan, " for I know — I feel that I shall never care for anything again. A cab from here to Richmond will cost a good deal; silver is what I want. I hope — oh, dear, where is my purse? I have dropped it — it is not in my pocket," and Percy stood transfixed with horror, as the full sense of his misfortune came upon him.

"What shall I do? What shall I do? Aunt Lucy would pay the cabman, I am sure; but I could not — I would not ask her. Oh, what a fool I have been to leave home at such an hour — on such a night. I dare not go back — I dare not go back."

To return home would have been the most natural and the shortest way out of his difficulty; but his foolish pride rose up stronger than ever, and prevented him once more from doing what was right.

So, heedless of the cutting wind he struggled on, afraid to retrace his footsteps, and unable to make up his mind to take a cab, since he must ask Mrs. Brown to pay the fare. This seemed an ignominious manner in which to arrive at the cottage, and so Percy could not prevail upon himself to do it.

It was now about seven o'clock, and the evening was so cold, that in spite of his warm coat and muffler, the boy shivered as he went along through the badly-lighted streets.

The day before, when he and Hugh had driven to Richmond, the roads were hard and clean; but the morning had brought a thaw, and, to add to the misery of this most wretched night, the pavements were thick with mud.

And so Percy wandered sadly on, his feet wet and cold, his head giddy from weakness and want of food.

"I must take a cab and get Aunt Lucy to pay the man for me," he cried, at last. "I do not like to do it but I must. I can walk no farther, and I dare not go home. Yes; the best thing to do is to take a hansom."

But now that he was willing to sacrifice himself and bear this degradation, there were no cabs to be seen. A feeling of despair came over him, and he grew so faint and weary that he longed to lie down there and then to rest.

"Oh, my God!" he cried, and tears of bitter sorrow rolled slowly down his cheeks, "do not leave me here to die in the cold. Send some one to help me. I am sorry now, oh, so sorry for my wicked conduct. Give me strength to return to my home, and I will bear patiently any punishment or humiliation that my father may think right to inflict upon me. I cannot walk to Richmond: there are no cabs to be had; and I now see what a wicked boy I have been. Oh, why did I leave my home? Why did I leave my home?"

Then, utterly humbled and subdued, the boy turned and walked wearily back towards Holland Park, hoping and praying that he might have strength to reach his father's house; for every step seemed as though it must be his last, and he trembled lest he should fall to the ground and die on the roadside. He had eaten nothing all day, and as he tottered along he grew so giddy that he had to lean for support against a lamp-post.

"Is there no one to help me — no one to pity me," he moaned, gazing about him in terror. "Am I to die here of cold and hunger? My God, help me! help me!"

But there seemed little hope of his prayer being heard. He was standing at a lonely part of the road, and, although there were houses on every side, yet not a creature passed him by, and he had neither strength nor courage to ring at one of the doors and ask for assistance.

It had grown colder and colder, as the evening advanced, and at last the snow came down in thick, white flakes.

Poor Percy became numb and frozen; his weak limbs refused to bear him any longer, and, scarcely knowing what he did, he reeled suddenly forward and fell to the ground.

But, just at this moment, a rumbling noise was heard in the distance, and a covered cart came down the road towards him. The driver, a hale old fellow of about sixty, was carefully wrapped up in a piece of sacking, in hopes of keeping the snow from penetrating his clothes; for it beat fiercely in upon him as he sat up in the front seat of his cart.

The horse seemed tired, and jogged slowly along, although his master did all he could to coax him into a fast trot.

As Percy heard the rattling of the wheels, his heart gave a bound, and raising his head with much difficulty, he called out in a weak voice:

"Help! help! Do not—oh, do not leave me to die here in the cold!"

At the sound of this piteous prayer, the driver stopped his horse, and, springing from his seat, caught the fainting boy in his arms.

Lifting him into the cart, he laid him tenderly on a bundle of straw, and gazed sadly at the pale, pinched face, and draggled golden hair.

Percy was now quite unconscious, and lay as white and still as though he were dead.

"A poor little hunchback, and a gentleman's son," remarked the old man, with a sigh. "But how comes he to be in such a plight? God grant that he may not be dead; but he looks very like it. Dear, dear, but it's a hard night for a delicate lad like this to be out. Truly we live in strange times;" and, taking his reins, he whipped up his horse to his fastest possible speed.

In a short time the old man drew up at the door of a wayside inn, and jumping down from his seat lifted the still unconscious boy in his arms; and leaving the horse and cart to take care of themselves, hurried into the house and laid the frozen child in front of a blazing fire.

The landlady, a thin, sharp-nosed woman, with a shrill voice, looked up in astonishment and disgust, as the snow-covered man appeared bearing his strange burden, which he deposited without leave or license upon her clean, bright carpet.

"What is that, Joe Bradley?" she questioned angrily.

"A little boy, ma'am, that I found nearly dead upon the roadside."

" Some miserable beggar, I suppose, who was too proud to go to the House, or too lazy to work !"

" No, ma'am, you are quite wrong," said Joe, rubbing the boy's hands within his own. " He is a gentleman's son, or I'm much mistaken."

" Well, gentleman or beggar, Joe Bradley, I wish you had taken him to the kitchen," she answered, sharply. " He's sopping with wet and covered with snow and mud. But, of course, you think it doesn't matter at all about spoiling my new carpet."

" Get me some brandy, ma'am, quick, ma'am," cried the old driver, pulling off the boy's muffler and coat as fast as his numb fingers would allow him. " He may die if we don't do something for him at once; he's just alive, poor chap, and no more. He's that cold and stiff, that only his heart's beatin' the least bit in the world, I'd say he was dead this minute."

" Not he. He's only in a faint and will come round fast enough. Let's hope he'll pay for the carpet he has spoiled," she cried, angrily ; and she bounded out of the room.

" If I had not been so frightened," muttered the old man, as he drew off Percy's wet boots and stockings, " I'd have gone on with him to

Richmond, where a true, kind-hearted woman would have welcomed the poor lad and done her best to bring him round. It's little this one cares for but her carpets and her—but, mercy me, her bark's worse nor her bite, I see, for here she comes with the brandy and a nice warm blanket to wrap the poor fellow up in."

The old driver knelt beside the unconscious boy, and taking the brandy from the woman's hand poured a few drops down his throat; then very gently rubbed his hands and bathed his face and head.

And, at last, to his great joy, the white lips quivered slightly, and, with a sigh, Percy opened his eyes and looked about him in surprise. But it was only for an instant; the brandy had done its work; the weary eyelids drooped and closed, and he fell fast asleep.

" Now he'll do; and thank God for it," cried honest Joe. " It would have broken my heart if the poor child had died; "and, in his delight, he shook the landlady by the hand, thanking her vehemently for having helped him to save the little wanderer's life.

"You're a good man, Joe Bradley," she said, softened in spite of herself by his kindly man-

ner; and if you had not spoilt my new carpet "—

"Now, don't you fret about your carpet,
ma'am, for it isn't one bit the worse," cried
Joe, "and, dear bless you, you and I mustn't
quarrel over a carpet after so many long years
of friendship; but where can I put the lad, so
that he may sleep in peace and quiet for the
rest of the night?"

"Roll him up in the blanket and put him on
the sofa, and I'll get a bed ready for him as
soon as I can," she said, more kindly. "I'll
make him comfortable for the sake of our old
friendship. You are a good Christian, and
you've taught me a lesson to-night."

The good-hearted old man was delighted to
hear her words, and thanked her warmly for
her kind assistance.

"You'll never have cause to regret this
night, ma'am," he said solemnly. "The Lord
will surely bless you, for taking in this poor
lad and saving his life."

"It's not much saving I'd have done, only
for you, Joe, I'm afraid. But now I must
go and look after his bed;" and she hurried
away.

"Her bark is truly worse nor her bite,"

thought Joe, with a smile. "An' thank God that it is so; but, indeed, there are many that way — but it's well to know — it's well to know."

Then rolling the warm blanket round the sleeping boy, this good Samaritan laid him gently on the sofa, lowered the gas, and went out to the yard to look after his horse and make him comfortable for the night.

CHAPTER XIV.

IN THE PARLOR OF THE RED LION INN.

PERCY slumbered peacefully on the sofa, and when Joe came back from the stables he felt sorry to disturb him.

"The lad seems very comfortable," he said; "but still I would like to get him tucked up in a bed for the night."

"Well, the bed won't be ready for awhile, Joe," replied the landlady. "I told the girl to air the sheets well and make everything snug. But come along now and have a bit of supper. You must be real hungry after your long drive. The boy won't wake up for many hours, so you need not be uneasy about him."

"I am very hungry, ma'am, and what is more, I'm uncommon dry," replied Joe, with a smile; "an' if you think there'll be no one comin' in to disturb the lad, I'll go with you right willin'."

"Disturb him? Law bless you! there'll be no one comin' in such a night as this. Folks is only too glad to stop at home when the snow comes down. But if a stray traveller did come in he wouldn't eat the boy; an' he's too sound asleep to wake up easily. So come along and take a pick."

"Very well, ma'am, since you are so good as to ask me, I'll go with you if you'll just lead the way," said Joe; and, with a kindly glance at the sleeping boy, he followed the landlady out of the room.

Now the mistress of the Red Lion could be very pleasant when she chose, and, what was more to the purpose, her larder was always well filled; so honest Joe rarely fared so well as when invited to join Mrs. Nipper at her cosy table.

The hot stew, for which the Red Lion was famous, tasted delicious after his cold drive from town; the beer was good and strong, the room warm and snug; and so, ere long the old man grew drowsy, and, forgetting his little charge upon the sofa, fell fast asleep in Mrs. Nipper's comfortable arm-chair.

"Poor old fellow, he's fairly done out," said the landlady, with a smile. "That's the best-hearted man I know anywhere, so I'll just leave him to enjoy his nap in peace," and away she bustled to get the rooms ready for the night.

Joe's sleep was long and undisturbed, Mrs. Nipper's occupation of an interesting and somewhat lengthy description; so Percy was left for many hours in peaceful possession of the parlor.

But suddenly, as the clock struck eleven, the lad was rudely wakened by loud shouting outside, and a moment later three men pushed their way into the room, shaking the snow from their coats, and calling to the servant for brandy.

. The girl implored them to go away to another room, as this was the landlady's best parlor, and that she would be angry at having her carpet spoiled by their muddy boots.

But the men laughed at the idea, and told her to be off and bring the brandy at once.

Too much frightened to urge them any more, Peggy ran away, and soon returned with a large bottle and some glasses; these she placed on the table, and fled off again, as fast as she could.

Drawing their chairs to the fire, the men

stuck their dirty boots against the shining bars, and, laughing wildly, declared they would soon make the old lady's grate nice and clean.

They were rough, uncouth-looking creatures, and Percy trembled with fear as the door closed upon Peggy, and he found himself alone with them.

But they did not see him; they sat with their backs well turned to the sofa, and so long as he kept quiet they were not likely to find out that he was there.

As the brandy went round, they grew talkative; and Percy soon discovered, from the stories they told, that they were men who went about from place to place, stealing and thieving whenever they could get the chance.

"It strikes me, Jimmy," said one of the ruffians, "that you're looking a bit down in the mouth. I was told yer were doin' a fine business, but yer don't look like it."

"No more I do," said Jimmy, sadly, "for I'm in a bad way. Times is very bad for men of our perfession. Vot with all the new inventions of locks and chains, an' the close watching of them perlicemen, there's no gettin' into a genelman's 'ouse where there's lots iv silver an' jewillery."

"Right yer are, Jimmy," answered one of his friends, a big burly fellow, with flashing black eyes and hooked nose. "But I had a rare piece of good luck this mornin' without puttin' myself 'bout or givin' myself hany trouble at all."

"Now, then, none o' yer long yarns, Moses, but tell us right off wot yer got," cried the others, impatiently.

"Well, then, yer must know that I've found a young 'oman wot's uncommon fond o' me," he answered, stroking his chin complacently.

"An' who cares whether yer 'ave or not?" cried Jimmy. "Leave the young 'oman alone an' tell us wot yer got an' where you got it from."

"Not so fast, my friend — not so fast," replied Moses, sipping his brandy. "If yer won't let me tell my story my own way — I won't tell it at all, so "—

"Well, go on then. But don't sit jawrin' there all night," cried the others, for they were all very curious to hear his tale.

"Well, then, as I said afore — I've a young 'oman," continued Moses, "an' she's a rare nice gal is my Mary Hann, an' wot's more she lives with a rich lady wot's got lots o' diamonds and jewels — an' my Mary Hann is from the country, an' she's nice an' soft like an "—

" Yer a lucky dawg, Moses," cried his friends; " for if she's nice an' soft she'll give yer a helpin' an' then — an' where there's diamonds and"—

" Don't hinterrupt me, genelmen, or I won't tell you no more," answered Moses, " and I've a rare good story to tell yer, if yer'll only listen."

" Why, man, we're all hears — so be quick with yer story; for that old warmint, Mrs. Nipper, will be turnin' us hout in a few minutes, I'll swaar."

" Right yer are, Jimmy, so I'll come to the pint in the twinklin' of a heye." And taking another glass of brandy he smacked his lips, and went on with his story.

" Well, yer must know that my Mary Hann 'as been stayin' with her missis for sometime back, at Olland Park, and it's there I come to know my pritty dear.   Well, in that 'ouse lives Sir Enery Randall, a rich an' great genelman, wot made 'eaps an' 'eaps of money in trade."

On hearing his father's name, Percy started up, and straining every nerve, tried to catch the man's words; but this was not at all easy,

as he dropped his voice from time to time
almost to a whisper.

"Now 'is son," continued Moses, "a queer
'unchback of a chap, 'ates my Mary Hann's
lady, an' wants to frighten her hout of the
'ouse, so wot do you think 'e does? Yer'll
never guess. Why pretends that some genelmen of our perfession got in by the winder, 'an
throws the siller about, an' "—

"Oh, golly, wot a pity we 'adn't been
there!" cried Jimmy and his comrade, in a
breath.

"That's just wot I said to my Mary Hann;
but listen. The young chap runs out screechin'
through the 'ouse — callin' murder an' thieves,
an' down comes 'is par an' the butler, with guns
an' pistols; so we'd 'ave got it 'ot I'm thinkin'!"

"Unless we'd got hout by the winder," suggested Jimmy.

"Oh, yes, but yer might 'ave been nabbed,"
said Moses. "But I've got far better nor
siller, without runnin' no risk or danger; for in
the confusion an' hurry, my Mary Hann remembered Moses, and when my lady ran hout of
her chamber to see wot was hup, she slipped in
by a little side-door, an' picked this little trifle
off her missis's dressing table," and far above

his head he held a beautiful diamond star that flashed and glittered as the light fell upon it.

With great difficulty the boy on the sofa suppressed a scream, for there in the ruffian's hand was the missing star, the loss of which, together with her bracelet, had so enraged his aunt, and caused her to accuse poor Hugh of heading the band of robbers supposed to have entered his father's house the night before.

"Oh," thought Percy to himself, "how wicked! how very wicked I have been! For had it not been for my wish to revenge myself on Aunt Lydia, Mary Ann would never, never have thought of stealing those diamonds."

The men by the fire were loud in their praise of the brilliants, and gazed at them with covetous eyes. Each one longed to have them for his own, and would gladly have wrested them from his comrade's hand had he dared to do so. But Moses was a strong fellow, and was pretty certain to have a knife or pistol somewhere about him. So they were obliged to content themselves with looking at the precious stones from a distance, whilst the lucky possessor went on with his tale.

"I'm glad to see yer can look at a thing 'o that kind an' not go a covetin' of it, my friends," he remarked, with a chuckle; "an' yer'll be glad to 'ear that no one in the 'ouse hever thinks of suspectin' my Mary Hann, an that the perlice is hafter quite a different party altogether — a young chap, called Hugh Brown, a newly discovered poor relation of Sir Enery's, wat he took in to be a companion to his son. I'm goin' to pop this star straight into pawn to-morrow mornin' and Mary Hann's to slip the ticket in among the youngster's clothes in 'is drawers, the minute 'e comes back to 'Olland Park; then all the danger'll be over for us, an' 'e'll be nabbed an' locked up straight away."

"Yer a darned lucky chap," cried his friends. "But don't forget yer pals when yer get that 'ere money."

"No fear 'o that, my lads, an' if yer'll come along to my diggin's to-morrow night, I'll give yer as good a supper as ever yer 'eard tell on."

"We'll be with yer sharp an' sure. But will yer kindly let us know where ye're livin' now?" said Jimmy, laughing. "Old Biddy Carew told me she wouldn't let yer into 'er 'ouse no more."

"So she did, the old warmint; cause I didn't pay for one week. But she'll be right down sorry when she 'ears I'm growin' rich. But not a penny she'll ever get for turnin' me hout."

"Ha, ha, ha," laughed the men. "That's the way to treat them; but tell us where's your crib now?"

"Well, for the present, I'm in a nice little nest at 22 Great Egerton Street, an' if yer'll come there to-morrow night, we'll 'ave some sport. But let's be off on our tramp. I 'car voices comin' along the passage — a man's voice, too. Maybe the old lady's got in the perlice," and, dashing off the remains of his brandy, Moses rushed out of the room, and was quickly followed by his two companions.

As the door closed behind them, Percy jumped up, and began to button his jacket, and look about for his boots.

All his pride and anger, his bitter thoughts and wicked longings for revenge, were gone now, and his one idea was to save Hugh from the humiliation of an arrest.

But he was so weak and faint, that he was obliged to lie down helplessly on the sofa; this pained him deeply, just when he wanted to be up and away on his errand of mercy.

The tears rolled down his pale cheeks, as he thought of the misery he was bringing upon his dear cousin, and in an agony of grief he prayed aloud, calling on God to help him, to show him some way out of this strange place, so that he might get to Richmond in time to save Hugh.

As the three men went out of the inn, they shut the front door with such a bang that Mrs. Nipper came running down to see what was the matter; and Joe jumped out of his chair with a bound, thinking the world must be coming to an end.

"Has that young prodigal of yours been running off with himself?" inquired the landlady, as she ran against the old man in the hall.

"Not he, indeed," cried Joe. "Why, he hadn't the strength to crawl over the floor— let alone run off in the snow, poor lad."

"Well, there hasn't been a creature in this house to-night, an' the door banged like thunder. I mistrusted that boy from the first, an' it's my belief he's after no good. Mr. Jack, the policeman, was just tellin' Peggy at the back door there, that there's some very bad characters goin' about. There was a set of burglars, he says, a friend told him about this mornin', that got into a grand house in Holland Park last night, and stole things right and left, frightened the life out of the gentleman's son, and did all kinds of dreadful things."

"Indeed," said Joe, "that's very bad news; and if I was you I'd keep my front door barred and bolted."

"Quite right, Joe, but just you go an' look after that lad. I shouldn't at all wonder if he was one of those robbers, and was only shamming weakness to get into a decent house for the night."

"Mrs. Nipper, ma'am, don't talk so much nonsense," said the old man, severely. "I'm surprised to hear it from a woman of your years."

"Well," she said, firmly, "you'll soon find I'm right. That boy's a bad lot, or my name's not Susan Nipper."

But kind-hearted Joe did not stay to argue the subject, and hurried away to the parlor; for, in spite of his indignant words to the contrary, he began to fear that the boy had, perhaps, rushed out again into the night. He was quickly re-assured, however, for before he opened the door, the sound of Percy's sad voice fell upon his ear; the heavy sobbing and fervent prayers touched the man to the heart, and filled him with pity.

As he entered the room, the boy staggered to his feet, and in broken accents implored him to take him on to Richmond at once.

" But, my poor lad," said Joe, kindly, " it is too late. It is now near twelve, and we could not get to Richmond before half-past one ; for my old horse is tired, and it is snowing hard. And, indeed, you are too weak and ill to go on."

" Never mind me," cried Percy. " If I die to-morrow it matters very little. But I must get on and save dear Hugh from prison."

" Save Hugh from prison ! Why, who is Hugh ? and who is going to put him in prison ?" asked the old man, humoring the boy, but feeling sure that his mind was wandering.

" Hugh Brown is my cousin, my best and dearest friend. And through my wicked conduct he will be arrested and put into prison, if "—

" Hugh Brown ! Hugh Brown going to prison ! Good little Hugh ! The best son and kindest lad that ever breathed ; but, of course, we do not mean the same Hugh ; that is not likely. The one I know of, lives in Holland Park with his cousin, a poor little humpbacked gentleman. But — I — you "— and Joe's honest face flushed, and his eyes grew sad, as he gazed at the little figure before him.

"Yes; I am the poor little humpbacked gentleman. I love my cousin, Hugh, dearly; and yet, because I tried to be revenged on a person whom I dislike, he is to be arrested and annoyed unless I arrive in time to prevent it."

And then Percy proceeded to tell the old man how his present misfortunes had come about. He told him how he had pretended that robbers had broken into his father's house; how his aunt had lost her jewels; and how he had overheard the man telling how and when they had been stolen, and the plot that had been laid for Hugh's ruin.

"I must warn Hugh," he cried, with tears in his eyes, "and urge him to fly. I should die of grief if he were put in prison, even for an hour. So, please, old man, take me on to Richmond before it is too late."

But Joe shook his head.

"My child, there would be no use going on to Richmond now: it is too late already; for if, as you tell me, all this happened early to-day, then, probably, your aunt sent to arrest the boy at once."

"No, no; I am sure she would not do that. Papa would not allow her."

"Well, then, the best chance of saving Master Hugh is to return home now and"—

"No; that would be foolish and impossible," cried Percy, wildly. "I could not go home; and it would be much better to warn Hugh and let him run away. Those men said the police would be sent after him soon. I must tell him to fly."

"Master Hugh will never do that; he is a brave lad and would rather face the danger than run away from it. He is innocent we know, and he knows himself, so why should he behave like a coward?"

"But it would. be only for a day or two, till things were explained," said Percy.

"I know he'd never run away," answered the old man firmly. "And if you love him, as you say you do, you must do what you can to save him. There is only one thing to be done, and that is, go back to your father's house, tell him all you have heard and seen to-night, and he will save Hugh, I am sure, for I know he is a good and honorable gentleman."

To this Percy made no reply, but sat for some moments in silence, his head buried in his hands, his whole body trembling with emotion.

At last he raised his face, which was deadly pale, and putting his hand into the old man's, said huskily, —

" You have been a true friend to me to-night.   You have saved me from certain death ; and now, I believe you wish to save me from never-ending remorse.   I will go back to my father ; if you can take me now, do, and God bless you."

"That is right.   That is brave and true," cried Joe.   " I'll take you back to Holland Park as fast as I can ; for Master Hugh is a great favorite of mine, and I'd dearly love to save him from harm."

" Do you know Hugh long ?" asked Percy.

" Not long if you reckon by months, for I only know him about six.   But since the evening when I took home his poor father in a faintin' condition I have loved that boy.   Bless his dear, good, warm little heart."

" Oh, are you the kind old man who carried poor Uncle Philip home ?" cried Percy, eagerly. " Hugh has often told me how good you were to them all."

" Good, indeed !" he replied ; " it's but little

I could do for them then; an' now that I have some money they've found their rich friends, and don't want my help. When I was ill an' laid up with rheumatics, Mrs. Brown was that kind an' looked after me so that — but there, it makes me cry to think of it," and he dashed his sleeve across his eyes. " Then, when my son in North Carolina, sent me home money, so that I needn't work no more, Mrs. Brown had grown rich and didn't want nothing from me."

" Have you come into a fortune, then?" asked Percy, absently; for his thoughts were far away, and he took but little interest in the old man's story.

" Well, not exactly a fortune, leastways not to the likes of you or your father; but a comfortable bit of money to an old fellow like me. I used to drive a cart and deliver parcels for Messrs. Toogood & Co.; now I do it on my own account. I bought my cart and my horse, an' I fetch and carry for a few good customers of my own. In this way I am my own master; and if I feel unwell and stay at home for a day, or go to bed early, why nobody bothers me. I was going on to Richmond with a lot of things for Mrs. Brown, when I found you on the road, and put up here for the night. But it seems to me I've been yarnin' too long about my own affairs, so let's hurry up and be off. I'd give all my money from North Carolina to find that thief, and clear Master Hugh from such a charge. I'll do it yet or my name's not Joe Bradley;" and turning away abruptly, he hurried out of the room.

With a heavy sigh, Percy rose from the sofa and began to prepare for his journey. His cheeks flushed and his heart beat wildly as he thought of the angry reception he would probably receive at his father's house. He was still so faint and weak that it took him a long time to fasten his boots, and he had only just finished when Joe returned to say that the cart was ready.

"Here is something to give you a little strength," he said, and placed a basin of hot soup before the famished boy.

Percy drank it eagerly, and then looked up with a grateful smile.

"You have been wonderfully good to me," he cried. "I feel better now, so pray let us start at once. If we are very late my father may be in bed; and I feel a great longing to speak to him to-night."

" And so you shall, my boy. The cart and horse are waiting at the door, and we can go when you wish. Lean on me and I will help you along. The horse is a little tired, but I'll make him take us to Holland Park as fast as he can. So, don't be uneasy, you'll see your good father to-night," said Joe, cheerfully; then, putting his arm round Percy, he almost carried him from the room.

It was bitterly cold, and the poor lad shivered as they passed out into the night. The old driver lifted him gently into the cart, laid him once more upon the straw, and covered him up with the warm blanket that he had taken from Mrs. Nipper's sofa.

Then clambering up to his seat in front of the vehicle, he drove off briskly through the snow and sleet.

CHAPTER XV.

SIR HENRY RECEIVES A SHOCK.

AS Percy fled from the library, his father uttered a deep groan, and, sinking into his chair, buried his face in his hands. He was completely overcome with grief, and felt strangely bewildered and perplexed.

At first the boy's story had seemed incredible; and, although he was annoyed that a son of his could stoop to tell a lie, even for the purpose of saving his friend, yet he hoped that Percy would see how wrong he was, acknowledge his fault, and beg his aunt's pardon.

Of Hugh's innocence he had not the slightest doubt.

But, when Percy persisted in declaring himself guilty of this wicked deceit; when he almost swore that he alone had laid and carried out this trick, in order to frighten Mrs. Torrens and make her leave the house, Sir Henry's anger and indignation knew no bounds, and he felt that no punishment would be too great for a child who was capable of acting in such a manner.

In the first flush of anger he did not remember how deeply Percy must have suffered before he brought himself to confess his sin so openly. He forgot the pale cheeks and quivering lips, the painful flushing and agonized look in the blue eyes; forgot everything, in fact, but that this boy, his own son, had behaved so shamefully, and, in a voice full of scorn, he bade him quit his presence at once.

But, as Percy fled away without a word, struck dumb with terror at his father's anger, Sir Henry's heart sank low, and he yearned to call the culprit back, and forgive him there and then.

But there stood Mrs. Torrens, cold and stern, ready to upbraid and reproach him if he should show any weakness in his dealings with his boy; there was Theo, the little sister, shocked and horrified at her brother's conduct; and there were the servants, who had all heard the story, and wondered at the strange confession.

And so the kind father did not dare to pardon the lad, as he longed to do, but felt bound to punish him severely, if only to give an example of his wisdom and justice. For this reason, then, he let him go away alone to his room, hoping, that in a few hours, he might arrive at some fixed idea as to what was the right kind of punishment to inflict upon him.

The servants returned to their work; Mrs. Torrens went off to pay a round of visits; but the unhappy father remained in the library plunged in deep and anxious thought.

Little Theo sat beside her father all day, afraid to speak, and yet longing to soothe and comfort him.

Never before had she seen him so much roused; never before had he spoken so harshly to Percy; and now, as she saw him sad and silent, she thought he must still be angry. So she kept very quiet, weeping softly behind her book, and wishing earnestly that she could find some way of putting things right again. At luncheon-time she hovered about him, tempting him to eat by bringing his favorite dishes under his notice. But all her efforts were in vain, and the dainties were removed untouched.

The day closed in, evening came on, and still the father and daughter sat together in the library.

Poor little Theo, worn out with weeping, dropped off to sleep as the daylight waned; but Sir Henry's thoughts were too busy for rest, and he sat gazing into the fire, with an anxious look on his face, quite unconscious of the passing hours.

At last, they were roused by the sound of the gong for dinner, and they started up and went into the dining-room without a word.

Mrs. Torrens was dining out; and Theo sighed as she thought of the happy evening they would have had together, had it not been for Percy's strange conduct. So long as the servants were in the room the child struggled bravely with her grief; but when they withdrew she broke down completely, and, leaning her head against the table, sobbed as if her heart would break.

Sir Henry had been so much occupied with his own thoughts that he had scarcely noticed poor Theo all day; but this sudden outburst alarmed him greatly.

"My darling child," he cried, "you must not weep so. Percy has been wicked, but you must not fret."

"Oh, forgive him, papa," she cried; "forgive him. Let him come now. I know he is very sorry; Percy always is, directly he has been wicked."

"But why doesn't he come and say so, Theo? I have never been cruel to him — he cannot be afraid of me."

"No, papa, no; but you said you could not bear to think of him as your son, and Percy is proud."

"Proud — poor lad — poor Percy. Ay, so he is; proud and sensitive; and I spoke so strongly in my anger at his wild, wicked conduct. But now, Theo, I long to take him in my arms, and tell him I forgive him, poor little motherless, afflicted boy. And yet I must punish him in some way, dear. Your aunt will expect it; she promised me not to send the police after Hugh, on condition that I did something. I know she thinks I should punish him, whether his story is true or not; and I suppose she is right."

"But, papa, dear, he has been punished enough, I am sure. Think of this long, weary day, without a creature to speak to. Think of him in his dark, lonely room, for no one has been near him. I know — I feel sure that he is really sorry now."

"He has certainly had a long, dreary day

of solitude; and if I thought he was really sorry, Theo "—

" I am sure he is, papa; let me go and see. Let me tell him now that you have forgiven him — pray, pray do," and clasping her hands round his neck, Theo raised her streaming eyes imploringly to his face.

Deeply touched by the child's earnestness, Sir Henry pressed her to his heart, and kissing her lovingly, told her to go and find her brother.

Full of joy, Theo sprang from her father's arms and ran down the hall to Percy's room.

" Percy, Percy," she called, knocking gently at first, and then a little louder; receiving no answer she thought he must have fallen asleep, and in hopes of awakening him rattled the handle somewhat noisily.

But, to her surprise, she found the door unlocked, so on she went down the passage and in through the crimson curtains. It was very dark, and she groped her way carefully along, calling continually to her brother, and wondering greatly where he could be.

But no one answered; and very much amazed at his silence, Theo stepped out into the hall again. Taking a candle (which had been set on the table ready for the night), she lighted it, and, walking on tip-toe, returned to Percy's room, where she peered about cautiously, expecting to find him fast asleep in some-out-of-the-way corner.

But Percy was nowhere to be seen. His bed in the alcove was empty; he was not on the sofa, nor yet in the arm-chair, and Theo's heart beat wildly as, holding the light first above her head and then down upon the ground, she gazed round her in every direction.

"How very strange," she cried. "Where can he be? He would never, never go up-stairs — at least, I am sure he would not. He does not know Aunt Lydia is out, and he would never risk meeting her. He must be here somewhere," and she resumed her search, looking anxiously about for some trace of the missing boy.

At last a nameless dread, an awful terror came over her, and dropping her candle she flew away from the room, back into her father's presence.

"He has gone, papa. Percy is not in his room," she cried in a trembling voice. "I cannot find him — I cannot find him; he has gone."

"Gone?" said her father, staring at her in astonishment. "Gone? You must be dreaming, child. Where could he go to? He must be in his room."

"He is not in his room, papa. I have looked everywhere, up and down. He must be gone — he must be gone."

"What a little goose you are, Theo. I suppose he has gone up to the drawing-room, or to Hugh's room. But I will go and help you to find him."

"Yes, do come, papa, for I feel so frightened; I am sure Percy is not in the house — I am, indeed."

"Nonsense, child; don't be so foolish," said her father, impatiently; but then he added, gently: "you are nervous, darling, after your unhappy day. Come along with me and we shall soon find out Percy's hiding-place."

But Theo was right. Percy was not in his own room, nor in any other room in the house, and the little girl wept bitterly at this strange disappearance of her brother.

Sir Henry was filled with dismay, and could not for some time believe that his son had really fled from his home.

But when he was at last convinced that such

was the case, his grief and anguish were too terrible to describe.

"What can I do, Theo? Where can the boy have gone to? Why was I so hard and stern to my poor erring child? Why did I not go to him and talk to him kindly? Where can the boy have gone? What will become of him on such a night?" and the strong man bent his head and wept.

"Papa, dear, do not fret so much," cried Theo, terrified at the sight of his tears. "Percy will soon come home again. And oh, papa, do you know what I think? I am quite certain Percy has gone off to Hugh."

"My darling, that is indeed a happy thought," said her father, hopefully. "I will send a telegram to the Cottage at once."

Handing over his little daughter to the tender care of good old Bridget, Sir Henry hastened off to the post-office himself, and sent a message to Hugh Brown, at Richmond. Then he went round the various police stations in the neighborhood, and gave a full description of the missing boy. It was late when he at last returned to the house, and on the hall table he found the answer to his telegram.

Seizing it eagerly, he tore it open, glanced

over its contents; then, letting it fall to the ground, turned away with a quick, sharp gasp of anguish. His lips quivered, his face grew ashy pale, and, staggering into the library, he sank upon the sofa, almost wild with anxiety and grief.

His last hope for his boy's safety was now gone; and he dared not think what had become of him on such a night.

Hugh's reply to the telegram was only too clear.

"Have not seen Percy since yesterday evening. Know nothing of his whereabouts," it said; and the father's brain seemed all on fire as he read the dreadful words.

"Where can the boy be? What in the name of heaven can have tempted him to leave his home?" he murmured, over and over again. "What will become of him without friends — for Percy never made a friend except Hugh. Without money — oh, God take care of my misguided child."

And the poor man's heart grew sick within him as his eyes fell on the little purse that had been found on the floor in the boy's room. The sight of this pretty toy caused him to start and shudder, for it made him realize very clearly the awful position in which the poor wanderer might be at that moment.

And so the night wore slowly on, and at one o'clock the unhappy father still paced up and down the library, seeking in vain to calm the wild beating of his heart, and longing for the morning, that he might resume his search for his child.

Thoughtful for others, in the midst of his troubles, Sir Henry told the servants to go to bed, whenever his sister returned from her party; and he warned them not to speak of Percy's disappearance in her presence, for that night at least.

His orders were strictly obeyed, and as Mrs. Torrens swept up the staircase in her silken robes, she knew nothing of the cruel anguish that her kind-hearted brother was enduring alone.

The lights were all put out; the doors and windows had long since been bolted and barred; but still Sir Henry remained in the library, brooding sadly over the strange events of the day.

All had been quiet and silent for a long time, when suddenly, the soft tinkling of a bell made the weary watcher start and tremble.   He listened nervously, but heard no more; so, sighing heavily, he resumed his restless walk up and down the room.

But again the sound fell upon his ear; this time so loud that he could no longer be mistaken; the visitor's bell rang clearly and distinctly through the house, and, uttering an exclamation of surprise, Sir Henry went down the hall and opened the door.

An old man, white with snow, stood on the steps, and out on the road was a covered cart, and a poor, tired-looking horse.

"I want to see Sir Henry Randall," said the man, his teeth chattering with cold.

"I am Sir Henry Randall. What do you want? Why do you come ringing here at this hour?" he asked, with emotion; for he hoped and yet dared not indulge in the thought, that, perhaps, this midnight visitor knew something of the missing boy.

"You shall soon know what I want, Sir Henry," said the old man, and turning, he waved his arm towards the cart.

But ere Sir Henry had time to question him further, a small figure was seen springing from the vehicle, and Percy ran across the snow to the hall-door. Throwing himself on the ground, he clasped his father round the knees, and gazed at him with streaming eyes.

"Father, dear father, forgive me," he cried; "punish me as you will; but, in God's name, forgive your unhappy son."

And his prayer was not made in vain. Forgetting his anger, his grief, and terrible sufferings, Sir Henry threw his arms round his child, and, whispering words of sweet forgiveness, pressed him to his heart.

CHAPTER XVI.

REMORSE.

SIR Henry's happiness was indeed great, when he saw his little son standing before him safe and well. But for some moments he could scarcely speak, and his voice was low and husky as he assured the boy that he forgave him from his heart.

Percy was deeply touched by the tender kindness of his father's manner, and felt that in all his life he should never be able to repay this love and affection that he deserved so little.

Honest Joe melted into tears at the sight of Sir Henry's emotion, and thanked God in his own simple way that he had been allowed to restore the young runaway to his father's arms.

Seeing them so absorbed in each other he turned away, and was going forth to seek a

lodging for himself and his horse; but Percy
saw his movement, and, starting forward, seized
hold of him and would not let him go.

"You must not leave this house to-night.
Do not let him, papa; he saved my life this
evening, so we must surely treat him well.
Only for him I should now be lying dead upon
the roadside."

"God bless you, my friend," cried Sir
Henry, grasping the old driver's hand. "I
am truly grateful to you, and know not how to
thank you for bringing my boy back to me. I
am sure that Percy will never forget you; for
though he is wild and foolish he has, I believe,
a loving heart. You must stay here to-night;
it would be quite impossible to get in anywhere so late."

"You are very kind, sir," said Joe, twisting
his hat nervously between his fingers; "but
you see I don't deserve any thanks. I only
did my duty when I brought the boy home. I
hope he'll never be so silly as to run away
again."

"Never again, Joe, never again," said Percy,
kissing his father's hand, and looking up lovingly into his face. "I've been very wicked
and revengeful; but I have suffered greatly. I

have learnt a lesson to-night that I don't think I am likely to forget."

"Poor lad, poor lad," cried his father, clasping him once more to his heart. "You have suffered bitterly, I am sure, and therefore I cannot bear to scold you, though you have caused me more anguish than you could ever imagine; but come, let us say no more about that. You are both half frozen with cold, and require to be warmed and taken care of. I must ring the bell now, and wake up the servants."

Sir Henry hurried them off to the library, and, making them sit down in comfortable chairs by the fire, rang the bell loudly.

They heard it clang and echo through the house, and, in a few minutes, the old butler came running up to see what was the matter. He started back in amazement, when his eyes fell upon Percy, seated in happy security by his father's side. This unexpected sight explained the violent ringing that had so startled and alarmed him, and his kindly face beamed with pleasure as he noted his master's look of extreme happiness and peace.

At a word from Sir Henry he marched good old Joe off to the servants' hall, where he did his best to make him comfortable, for he felt grateful to him for saving little Percy, whom he dearly loved, in spite of his many faults.

The coachman was roused from his slumbers, and the poor horse was, at last, allowed to take his rest in a snug stable, whilst the cart was stowed away in the coach-house amongst the carriages.

A tempting supper was soon brought up for Percy, but he could not eat a morsel. He was greatly excited, and hung about his father as if he could not bear to leave him for an instant.

Sir Henry implored him to go to bed if he was quite certain that he could not eat; but the boy refused to do this, declaring that he could not rest until he had told him all his adventures.

"But don't you think they might keep till morning, Percy, dear? You seem so tired and weary."

"No, no, papa; I could not rest until I have told you everything," cried his son; and then he gave him a hurried account of all that had occurred since the moment when he had left the library in disgrace.

"It is the most extraordinary story I ever heard," cried Sir Henry. "To think of the rascal boasting of Mary Ann's wickedness. But I am glad we have a clew, for we may now be able to recover your Aunt Lydia's jewels for her."

"I don't care a pin about that," cried Percy; "but I am glad that she can no longer blame Hugh, and call him a thief."

"She would not do that now, any way," answered Sir Henry. "At least, I think I have persuaded her that she was wrong. She wore the bracelet and star at a dinner-party, and did not take them off till quite late — long after Hugh had left the house by her own orders; so, if she will only believe that there were no robbers here — that no stranger entered the place, and that your story is true, she must know "—

"Father, father, do not remind me of my wickedness," exclaimed Percy, flushing painfully. "I hate to think of it."

"But you must think of it, my boy," replied his father, gravely. "You have sinned, and, although I have forgiven you, I am greatly afraid there is still much suffering in store for you."

"But how? why?" asked Percy, in a quick, startled tone.

"You have brought it all on yourself, my poor child,"·said Sir Henry, sadly. "If we arrest Mary Ann; if we pursue this man and get back the diamonds, you must, I feel certain, appear in court as a witness; you must state the case and tell the story as you told it to me."

"Oh, I could not do it; I could not do it. Let them keep the jewels. Aunt Lydia can do very well without them."

"No, no; we must do no such thing. That would be wrong and cowardly in the extreme," said his father, sternly. "You must do all you can to atone for your wicked conduct, and help your aunt to recover the diamonds she has lost. You must do what you can, Percy, and do it like a man."

"But then every one will know how I tried to be revenged, how badly I behaved to Aunt Lydia," moaned Percy, rocking himself backwards and forwards on his chair. "I cannot do it, father; I'd rather die than do it."

"My boy, my dear boy, you must not talk so wildly," cried Sir Henry, terrified at the agonized despair in the child's voice. "It will not be as terrible as you seem to suppose. Try to think of this ordeal as a punishment for your conduct, which you know was wicked, and which you regret so much. Try to bear it patiently and "—

"I can't—I—can't—I—," and, quite suddenly, without any word of warning, Percy fell, fainting, at his father's feet.

"The poor lad is quite done out. How stupid of me to let him talk so much, after such a day of misery," exclaimed Sir Henry; and, raising him tenderly, he laid him on the sofa, and bathed his head and face with cold water.

For some moments, and they seemed like hours to the anxious watcher, Percy remained unconscious; but, at last, he opened his eyes, and, with a heavy sigh, looked about the room in a weary, uncertain manner. He seemed to have forgotten where he was, and all the strange incidents of that eventful day.

"I feel tired, papa. Don't you think I might go to bed?" he asked, softly; "but you must help me, for I feel—so—so—that I can't move—I—," and his head dropped back, helplessly, on his pillow.

Very much surprised at this sudden change, Sir Henry carried him down to his room and put him to bed. As he helped him to undress, he noticed, with alarm, that his cheeks and hands were hot and burning; but when the weary eyes closed in peaceful sleep, he felt certain that all was well.

Then, kissing the boy tenderly, upon lip and brow, he stole away to his room to seek the rest he required so much after his day of trouble and anxiety.

The next morning, very early, before the servants had begun their round of daily duties, Hugh went briskly up to the front door and rang the bell. It was speedily opened for him by the maid, who was going forth to wash the steps.

He bade her "good-morning," and questioned her closely about Percy and his mysterious disappearance. The girl told him of her young master's return, and Hugh was filled with joy at the good news.

There was no fear of meeting Mrs. Torrens at that early hour, so Hugh entered the hall and hurried along to Percy's room. He walked very lightly lest he should wake the sleeping boy, — for he knew his cousin was a late riser, and expected to find him still in bed.

But, as he approached the apartment, he was surprised to hear loud shouting and talking going on within. Full of wonder, he raised

the curtain, and was about to make some laughing remark, when he suddenly stopped short,
appalled by the sight that met his eyes.

Sir Henry knelt in silent despair by Percy's
bed, his arms thrown round the boy, who
shouted and screamed in the wildest manner.
His eyes were strangely bright; his cheeks hot
and burning; he tossed madly to and fro upon
his bed, and would surely have flung himself
out upon the floor had not his father been near
to protect and restrain him.

Poor little Theo crouched in a distant corner, sobbing and moaning, calling earnestly to
God to have pity on them, and make her
brother well again.

" Theo, Theo, tell me what has happened?
What is the matter with Percy?" whispered
Hugh, creeping across the room to the weeping
girl.

" I am so glad you have come, Hugh; I am
so glad you have come," she said, and she flung
herself into his arms with a cry of joy.

" But what is wrong, Theo? Why does
Percy throw himself about like that?"

" I don't know why," she sobbed. " Poor
fellow, he seems so strange; he's mad, I think.
Papa says it's fever; but, oh! I'm glad you

have come. The poor boy has done nothing
but call for you all morning. We sent Grey
for you and the doctor; but he hasn't had time
to get to Richmond yet, and — and it was very
good of you to come off so fast."

"I was very anxious to hear about Percy,"
whispered Hugh. "I was so frightened when
I got uncle's telegram last night, and I came to
see if he had come home, as soon as ever I
could."

"Yes, he has come home, as you see; but —
but — I don't know when or how he came; for
it must have been after I went to bed. This
morning early, Kapes told me he was here and
very ill. I ran down to see him, and he has
been like that ever since I came in. Poor papa
doesn't know what to do."

"Save me! save me!" cried Percy, clutching wildly at the bedclothes; "those men —
look at their glaring eyes, ah! they are coming; they are coming. Don't tell Aunt Lydia —
the diamonds — Hugh, Hugh. He is good;
he's good; don't send him away; he's my
cousin; my best friend; he'll hear of my
wickedness, my lies, my — but I'll be revenged; I'll make her"— And then, with a
sigh, he fell back, exhausted, on his pillow.

" What pain, what pain," he murmured, presently, turning his head, restlessly, from one side to the other. " What fearful pain, and it's all because I was cruel, and — no, no; it's Aunt Lydia's fault; why did she treat Hugh so badly? She shall not get her jewels, ha! ha! I'm glad, but, oh! the sorrow of it all. Papa says I must tell; and they'll laugh and point. Oh! I couldn't do it. No, no, I'd rather die; but, no; for I should never see my dear mother then. God have pity, mercy, forgive," and, closing his eyes, he sank into a stupor.

Dreadfully shocked at his cousin's unhappy condition, Hugh remained standing in silence in the middle of the room, his arm thrown round Theo, who started and trembled at every word her brother uttered.

Sir Henry was wild with grief; and in his extreme agitation scarcely knew what to do. He had sent for the doctor some time before, but he had not arrived, and the poor man was sadly troubled at this delay.

When, at last, he observed Hugh, he signed to him to approach, and, as he held out his hand to draw him to his side, the boy seized it and covered it with kisses.

Touched by this token of affectionate sympathy, Sir Henry put his arm around him and pressed his lips to his forehead.

" My dear lad," he said, in a husky voice, " it was very good of you to come. You have been injured and insulted, and I am very sorry that you were treated so shamefully; but I can see that you bear no ill-will; that you have forgiven Mrs. Torrens."

" Oh, yes," answered Hugh, quickly. "She thought I had prompted Percy to play a wicked trick; and, had I done so, she would have been quite right to send me home as she did; but I did not, uncle; indeed, I did not."

" No, my boy, I am quite sure you did not. You are good and forgiving, Hugh : would that poor Percy had been the same. His aunt affronted him, was unkind and insulting; and he could not bear it, as you have done. He tried to frighten her, to be revenged, and see what his passionate desires have brought him to. He is dying, I know — I feel sure, and his whole soul is torn with the anguish of remorse."

" No, no, he cannot — he must not die. Let us pray that he may not die. God will not take him away till he truly repents — till he is really sorry for his wicked conduct," cried Hugh, earnestly; and he fell on his knees weeping and praying.

The heartbroken father tried to follow the boy's simple prayer for mercy, as he knelt close to his suffering child, whose frequent groans and cries of pain filled his heart with sorrow; and Theo's little voice joined Hugh's in his fervent supplications, her sobs growing fainter as she repeated the holy words.

At last it seemed as though God had, indeed, listened to their entreaties, for Percy grew quieter, and after some time fell asleep.

This happy change in his little son was a great relief to Sir Henry, and made him more hopeful of his recovery. Raising Hugh from his knees, he pressed his hands warmly within his own, saying:

"God bless you, dear boy. You have been a great comfort to me, and your prayers have done poor Percy good. Stay beside him now, whilst I go in search of Bridget."

"My mother would come, uncle—pray send for her," cried Hugh. "She is such a good nurse—so gentle and kind, and I know she would be so glad to come."

"That would be a blessing for my boy; he

loves his Aunt Lucy dearly," said Sir Henry, smiling. "Yes, I will send and ask her to come. She can bring Susie with her — Theo will be glad to have her."

"Yes, indeed I would," said Theo; "and, oh, how delightful to have Aunt Lucy in the house."

"Delightful for us, but a trial for her," said her father. "And now, Hugh, I shall leave you with Percy for a minute or two. He is quiet and peaceful, thank God, so there is no fear. If he wakes, ring, and I will come at once. Come, Theo, you must not stay here. I cannot have my daughter ill, too." And, taking the little girl by the hand, he went away, leaving Hugh in charge of the sleeping boy.

But Percy's sleep was of short duration, and to Hugh's horror he started up suddenly and gazed at him wildly, not knowing in the least who he was.

"I want Hugh," he shrieked. "I must speak to Hugh — I must tell him to fly. But don't let Aunt Lydia know, or she'll put him in prison. Call Hugh, I say. When I see him my head will be cooler — and oh, how it burns — how it burns."

" Percy, dear, I am here beside you," said Hugh, gently, laying his hand upon Percy's as he spoke.

" Who are you? You are not Hugh. Go away, I know who you are — you are the wretch that stole the diamonds; but the police will soon get you! ha, ha, ha! But give me that star — give it to me I say, or I'll — I'll make you," and, springing to the side of the bed, he seized Hugh by the throat.

Terrified at this sudden attack, Hugh did his best to free himself gently from the frenzied grasp, for he was afraid that he should excite the patient still more if he threw him off too roughly.

But very soon the fingers relaxed their hold, and Percy fell back panting for breath.

Hugh burst into tears as he watched the suffering child, and he trembled to think that if another paroxysm came on, he might not have strength to keep him in his bed.

At last, to his intense relief, the door opened, and Sir Henry entered the room with the doctor.

The latter approached the bed, and placing his hand upon the burning brow, uttered an exclamation of surprise and disgust. Seizing a pair of scissors that lay on the table near, he raised Percy's golden curls, and cut them all off, close to his head.

Sir Henry started, and made a movement as though to stop the cruel hands; but the doctor looked at him quietly over his spectacles, and proceeded calmly with his work.

"That is well done," he remarked, with satisfaction, as the last long tress fell from his fingers to the ground. "It is worth any money to be rid of that load, though we shall have to shave him by and by."

"Was it quite necessary to cut off all his beautiful hair?" asked Sir Henry, regretfully; "the poor boy liked it."

"Necessary!" cried the doctor. "My dear Sir Henry, your son is suffering from an attack of brain fever. We must keep his head as cool as possible."

He then gave many directions as to how the patient was to be treated, advised them to watch him constantly; not to allow too many persons in the room at once; and, above all, let nothing be said or done that could excite or agitate him. The good doctor then hurried away, promising to return in a few hours.

That day was a terrible one for all who

loved the fever-stricken child. One moment he was wildly delirious, the next he lay back on his pillow, in an almost death-like stillness.

When Mrs. Brown received her brother-in-law's telegram, announcing Percy's illness, she packed up a few necessary articles, handed Susie over to the care of her little maid, and set out for Holland Park.

Arrived there, she took her place at once in the sick room; and it was a great comfort to Sir Henry to see how tenderly she nursed the boy, and how well she seemed to understand all that was required.

Hugh sat in silence at the foot of the bed, slipping away, when Percy grew quiet, to carry a word of comfort to the little sister, who was not allowed to go near the patient.

When Mrs. Torrens heard that Percy was ill, she was deeply grieved. She did not love the boy, for he had been a thorn in her side for many years; but Sir Henry had always been good and affectionate, and for his sake she was really sorry. She offered to go to his room and nurse him; but knowing how much Percy disliked her, his father would not allow her to think of such a thing. He refused her offer, therefore, gently but firmly, thanking her sincerely for her kind intentions.

She then said she was going to Brighton for a time, and would be very glad to take Theo with her.

To this Sir Henry would readily have given his consent, as it pained him to see his little daughter wandering so sadly through the house; but she implored him to allow her to stay at home and comfort him, and take care of Percy when he began to get better.

She looked so sweet and tender as she made her request, that her father caught her in his arms, and said she should do exactly as she liked.

"Then I shall certainly stay at home, papa dear. I should be so unhappy away from you all."

Very angry at the child's decision, Mrs. Torrens flounced out of the library, and went off to make her preparations for her journey.

She went away that afternoon, and no one was much grieved at her departure.

In his anxiety about his son, Sir Henry quite forgot to tell his sister the strange story that Percy had overheard in the parlor of the Red

Lion Inn ; and so it happened that Mary Ann, the dishonest maid, remained with her mistress, and accompanied her on her sudden trip to Brighton.

CHAPTER XVII.

CONVALESCENCE.

FOR six weary days, Percy remained in the same alarming condition; at one time quiet and exhausted, at another raving in the wild delirium of fever.

On the seventh day, however, he grew gradually calmer, and at last fell into a deep sleep.

Sir Henry and Hugh were rejoiced at the sight, and sat for a long time in silence by his bed.

But fatigued as they were by watching and anxiety, they soon followed the invalid's example, and slumbered peacefully in their armchairs.

Percy slept for several hours, and, when he opened his eyes, he looked curiously round the room. He called for Hugh, as he had so often done before, and in an instant his cousin was by his side.

"Here I am, Percy dear," cried Hugh, delighted at the quiet sound of the patient's voice. "How do you feel?"

"I feel weak, so weak, Hugh; but the pain has gone. I am glad you have come, for I wanted to talk to you. Do you know what I did?"

"Yes; I have heard; but you must not talk so much; you are to be kept very quiet. The doctor says talking is bad for you."

"Have I been ill?" asked Percy, languidly. "I feel so strange and I have been having such bad dreams. I am so glad they are over, for they made my head ache and burn so."

"You have been ill, Percy, very ill," said Hugh, gravely; "but you are better now; drink a little of this and try to go to sleep again."

"That is very nice," he murmured, as Hugh put some iced lemonade to his lips. "It is so good of you to stay with me, Hugh, when I have been so cross and disagreeable to you; but, please, do not leave me; I get so frightened when I am left alone."

"You have not been alone for an instant, Percy; some one was always with you; only you did not know us."

"I knew you all quite well," answered Percy; "but I was so taken up with those horrid dreams, that I could not speak to you. I thought I was in court, Hugh, swearing about those dreadful men and the diamond star, and as I told my story every one laughed at me, and pointed their fingers at me, and there were great red tongues, with '*liar*' written on them, stuck out at me from all the corners. Oh, it was terrible—terrible," and the boy shuddered at the recollection.

Hugh was alarmed to see Percy growing excited again, and did what he could to soothe him.

"Try and forget those dreams, dear," he whispered; "think of something pleasant and go to sleep again."

"Very well, I will," said Percy, smiling faintly; "I'll think of you, Hugh, for you are the pleasantest thing I know."

"So long as you are happy I don't care what you think about," answered Hugh, and he shook up his cousin's pillows, and gave him another refreshing drink.

And as Percy was very weak, and felt exhausted with the effort he had made, he gladly took Hugh's advice; closing his eyes he turned away his head, and soon dropped off to sleep again.

Sir Henry was overjoyed to hear his son talk so sensibly to Hugh, and he longed to run forward and clasp him to his heart; but the doctor had warned them not to excite him when he first awoke; so, the loving father restrained himself and kept quietly out of sight whilst the above conversation was carried on between the two boys.

All danger was now at an end, and from that day Percy began to get well.

But it was difficult to regain the strength he had lost, and for many months Sir Henry watched his child with renewed tenderness and care.

And Percy was deeply touched by his father's kind forgiveness, and did all he could to show him how grateful he felt, and how dearly he loved him.

But yet the lad did not regain his happiness with his health, slowly as it came.

There are certain sins, dear children, that, no matter how generously they are forgiven by those around us, always bring their own punishment. And this was what Percy felt keenly, as he looked back upon the past.

His father had forgiven him, Hugh and Theo were more loving and attentive than ever, and yet he could not forgive himself; his heart was full of remorse.

During the long weeks of his convalescence he had pondered deeply over all the actions of his life, and especially over his conduct towards Mrs. Torrens. Hugh and he had talked about it, time after time, and his great desire was to atone for his shameful behavior, and obtain his aunt's forgiveness.

But this was difficult to accomplish. Mrs. Torrens considered that she had been badly treated by her brother and his son, and vowed that she would never enter the house again.

Had she made that resolution some months before no one would have tempted her to break it; but now Percy was seized with a great longing to have her back, that he might prove how truly he repented his wicked conduct.

And anxious as he always was to please his boy in every way, Sir Henry wrote to his sister, asking her to come to them, if only for a week.

But she could not be persuaded to change her mind, and wrote a long tirade against Percy and his wickedness. The story of the

star and the men at the Red Lion Inn she declared to be a pure invention; that nothing
would induce her to believe a word that such a
boy said; and that, until she had better proof
of Mary Ann's dishonesty, she intended keeping her in her service.

This letter was handed to Sir Henry, one
evening, as he sat by the sofa in his son's room.
Glancing over its contents, he crushed it between his fingers, and thrust it hurriedly into
his pocket. The cruel words had wounded
him deeply, and he wished to save Percy as
much as possible from any annoyance; but the
boy noticed the look of pain upon his father's
face, and guessed directly what it was that
troubled him.

"Papa, dear," he said, holding out his little
thin hand, "give me that letter, please. It is
from Aunt Lydia, I am sure, and I want to see
what she says about me."

"It would only pain you to read it, Percy;
and you are too weak to bear vexation just yet;
so do not ask to see this to-day."

"Father," said Percy, gravely, "you wish
to spare me all trouble, I know; but I am not
sure that you are right. A little suffering is
good for us in this world. Those who have

something to bear, and bear it well, are always the best and most lovable."

" My dear boy !"

" Yes, father ; I am certain they are. I have learned many things lately from the good people who have come to visit me ; and that is one. Look at Aunt Lucy, how sweet and good she is ! Look at Hugh, whose childhood was passed in poverty and trouble ! and then look at me, who have had everything I wanted, and always tried to get away from the least little thing that was disagreeable. See how different we are."

" Yes ; perhaps you are. But still I do not see why you should give yourself unnecessary pain, dear child."

" But it is not unnecessary, papa," urged Percy. " I have sinned deeply, and it is only right that I should bear the consequences. Therefore, you must let me see Aunt Lydia's letter, so that I may know her true opinion of me."

" Well, Percy, if you really wish it, here it is," replied his father, sadly. " I am sorry for your sake and her own, that she cannot be more kind and forgiving." And with great reluctance he handed the letter to his son.

Percy smoothed out the crumpled paper, and shading his face with his hand, began to read it slowly and attentively: and as he read, and the full meaning of his aunt's words grew upon him, his pale cheeks flushed, and the tears started to his eyes.

"She is very cruel," he cried at last, "very, very cruel; but, alas, dear father, I deserve every word she says."

"She was wrong to write in such a manner," exclaimed Sir Henry, angrily. "I told her all you have suffered, how sorry you are, and she should have forgiven you at once." And taking up the letter he flung it into the fire.

"Oh, papa, you should not have done that," said Percy. "It would have been better to have kept it, until I could have proved to her that I am not quite so bad as she believes me to be; then I could have burned it joyfully."

"I have no patience with her, and I cannot understand her hard cruelty."

"But, really, papa dear, it is no wonder she is angry, for I did behave very badly," said Percy, putting his arm round his father's neck. "you know how difficult you found it to forgive me at first — you who love me so dearly. And then you must not forget that she blames me for the loss of her diamonds; and, unfortunately, she is right; for if I had not made up that horrible story about the robbers, Mary Ann would never have dared to touch either star or bracelet."

"That is all quite true, dear; but why doesn't she believe what I tell her? Why doesn't she watch Mary Ann, search her boxes, and dismiss her?"

"Yes; I wish she would before it is too late. She gave the star to that man; but then, what did she do with the bracelet, I wonder? If Aunt Lydia would only take some trouble, she might find out all about it, and, perhaps, get her diamonds back again."

"She is shamefully hard on you, dear boy, and I feel grieved beyond measure at her conduct," said Sir Henry. "No matter what she lost, she had no right to speak of you as she has done. But, my dear lad, I do hope this will be a great lesson to you, and that you now see how terrible a thing it is to give way to a revengeful spirit. Just see what sorrow it has brought into your life."

"Yes, papa; indeed I do," cried Percy, earnestly.

"You acted a lie — a series of lies — and

now nothing that I can say will persuade your aunt that you are not a thorough liar and story-teller. It will be very hard to make her change her opinion — very hard."

"Yes, I am afraid it will," sighed Percy. "But the worst of it is, that I deserve that she should despise and think ill of me. How can she know that my illness has changed me? How can she know that I have truly repented, and that if she came here again I would treat her with every respect?"

"She might give you the chance, anyway, my dear child."

"Yes; I wish she would. It would make me so happy to show her how different I am now. But about the star, papa? Did you send to the right place? To the street I heard the fellow mention?"

"I sent to the very street you told me of, Percy; but no such person was to be heard of in that locality. The detectives have been on the look-out ever since, but have never seen any one at all like the man you described."

"That is too bad," cried Percy. "For until I find the diamonds, Aunt Lydia will never forgive me, I am sure. If I could get them she might come back, and then I could show her how sorry I am for my past wickedness, and prove to her that I am not a liar, as she seems to think," and the boy's lips began to quiver, and his eyes were wet and shining.

"No trouble shall be spared — no stone shall be left unturned till the diamonds are found," said Sir Henry, firmly. "But are you willing to do your part, Percy? Will you be ready, if necessary, to appear before a crowded court, if we can lay our hands on this ruffian?"

"Father, I am ready to do what is right. Hugh and I have talked it over many times, and he has managed to make me think of doing so, without that awful fear of it that I used to have."

"Hugh is a good, brave lad," said Sir Henry, warmly.

"That he is : good, brave, and clever; just the sort of a son you should have, papa, instead of a wretched creature like me," said Percy, in a choking voice.

"My dear, dear child, you must not speak like that, and give way to such morbid fancies," replied his father, laying his hand gently on his head. "You are more dear to me than fifty Hughs. You are my own little son; and, in spite of your faults, Percy, I love you most tenderly. Your gentle patience during this long illness; your keen anxiety to repair the mischief you have done, fill me with happiness, and make me certain that you will be very different in the future to what you have been in the past. I love Hugh. I think him a good, clever lad, and he is my nephew; but he is as nothing to me when compared with you, and the great love I bear you. Now, are you satisfied?"

"Yes, papa; indeed I am—more than satisfied. Your words have made me very happy," and, springing from his couch, Percy flung himself into his father's arms and kissed him long and lovingly.

"That is right; and now, my boy, you must lie down again, or we shall have you quite ill, and unable to go for your drive to-morrow. If you do not keep very quiet I shall go for your Aunt Lucy."

"No, no, papa; let poor Aunt Lucy rest for awhile. She looked so tired this afternoon. I'll be very good."

"Then I shall leave Aunt Lucy in peace; but it would be a shocking thing if I allowed you to talk too much and you got ill again."

"No fear of that," cried Percy, gayly. "I

feel ten times stronger for having had such a cheering conversation; but, oh, father, if we could only find those diamonds, I would go to Aunt Lydia with them myself, and then she would be obliged to forgive me."

"You shall win that forgiveness, my dear lad, if I can possibly manage it; but you must have patience, and not expect everything to be found out at once."

Here the sound of footsteps was heard approaching the room, and Sir Henry made a movement as though to prevent the intruders from coming in.

"You cannot be disturbed now, Percy; you are quite too tired."

"No, no, papa; indeed I am not," said the boy, eagerly; "pray, let my visitors come in."

"Well, if you wish it," said Sir Henry, and he returned to his seat by the sofa.

"May I come in, Percy?" asked a cheery voice, and Hugh's bright face appeared in the doorway.

"Come in? I should just think so," cried Percy. "Why, Hugh, you are as welcome as the flowers in May."

"That's good news," said Hugh, laughing. "You seem very lively, Cousin Percy; but, oh, please, Uncle Henry, Joe Bradley is in the passage. He doesn't like to come in until you ask him to do so."

"Not like to come in? What nonsense!" cried Sir Henry. Then going into the passage he shook the old man warmly by the hand. "My dear Mr. Bradley, pray come in. My son is much better and most anxious to see you."

"Is it really Joe? Dear old Joe?" shouted Percy, jumping up off the sofa. "Have you any news for me, Joe? Have you news of the diamonds?"

"Lie down, Percy, or I shall not allow you to ask another question," cried his father.

"Very well, papa," replied the boy; and he lay back at once upon his cushions. "Now, Joe, tell me quick; for I know — I feel sure by the twinkle of your eye, that you have something important to tell me. And Hugh, there, looks so knowing. Oh, please be quick and tell me all about it!"

"Yes, Master Percy," said the old man; and he took a chair and seated himself by the boy's side. "You are quite right; I have news — a wonderful piece of news to tell you."

CHAPTER XVIII.

JOE BRADLEY'S STORY.

"I KNEW I was right," cried Percy, gayly; "so out with the news, Joe — out with the news."

"Well, now, Master Percy, I've a story to tell," said the old man; "but you must just let me tell it in my own way, quietly and peacefully; for if you don't, I'll take Sir Henry away and tell him alone in his library."

"No, no; pray don't do that," cried Percy. "I promise not to hurry or interrupt you, so please stay where you are."

"Well, then, you all know that ever since I met you that night, Master Percy, and heard that Mrs. Torrens had lost her diamonds, I've been in a terrible way to find them. Not that I cared much for the lady, but because it had been whispered that Master Hugh here had something to do with the stealin' of them.

So, for the sake of his dear mother, who has been so good to me, I vowed that I'd never rest till I found out who took them — even if it took all the money that I got from North Carolina to do it. An' so I made up my mind that I'd keep my eye on Mary Ann, the lady's maid; for I believed Master Percy's story about the man and the star."

"Thank you, Joe, old friend," whispered Percy, with a grateful smile.

"Well, as I believed that story, I thought it best to keep my eye on Mary Ann, as I said before; and as she was in Brighton, I went to Brighton, — for, on account of the money from North Carolina, I'm pretty well my own master. I took my old horse and cart with me; and, thanks to some introductions from my friend, Mrs. Nipper, I got some work to do, that kept my pot a boilin'. An' then I set to watch the young woman as well as I could. When she went out of an evenin', I went out, an' so on. But I saw nothin' for a long time, an' at last I grew rather tired an' did not go near her for two or three days. Then, this afternoon, I went up to the hotel where she an' her Missis were stayin', an' asked the man at the door if Miss Mary Ann Jenkins was within.

"'Oh, she's gone,' says he; 'she an' her lady had a fight, an' she's gone; she left here about half-an-hour ago, an' I believe she's off to to London this very day.'"

"To London? Then Aunt Lydia has sent her away at last," cried Percy; "did she find out that she'd taken the diamonds, after all?"

"I think not, sir," said Joe, dryly; "but no interruption, please, or"—

"All right, Joe," laughed Percy; "but go on, please, your story grows extremely interesting."

"Well, when I heard that my brave Mary Ann was off to London, says I, 'Joe, you'd better go to London too; this is Saturday evenin', an' you won't have any work to do till Monday; an' there's many a friend will be right glad to see your old face at their table on Sunday.'"

"I should just think so," cried Hugh; "why, you're looked upon as a regular good fairy down where you used to live."

"Aye, aye, Master Hugh," said the old fellow smiling; "the old folks is wonderful grateful for any little bit of kindness. But to return to my story; off I went to the station; took my ticket; looked up an' down, but no

Mary Ann was to be seen; 'never mind,' says I, 'you've took your ticket, Joe, so go to London you must.'"

"And a very good thing you did," remarked Hugh; "for if you hadn't" —

"No interruption, Master Hugh. Well, Sir Henry, I went to the train; stepped into a third-class carriage, an' lo! an' behold! there was Miss Mary Ann sittin' waitin' for me as it were."

"'How do you do, Miss Jenkins?' said I, nice and civil like, 'an' where are you off to?'

"'I'm Miss Jenkins no longer,' she cried, 'I'm Mrs. Samuel Moses; I'm off to America with my husband to-morrow.'

"'Indeed, ma'am,' says I; an' then I thought sadly: 'you're done for, Joe, you're done for; what about the diamonds now?'"

"Why, Moses was the name of the man that had the star," cried Percy; "why didn't you ask Mary Ann about the bracelet?"

"Why didn't I ask her if she had it in her pocket, is it, Master Percy?" said Joe, laughing. "Well, I don't think there would have been much use in that sort of a question, leastways, if you expected a truthful answer: however, I didn't ask it, but sat an' talked quite friendly-like, as the train whirled us along on our way to London; an' then we got precious thick, an' she told me how angry Mrs. Torrens was, when she found she was married on the sly, an' how she gave her notice to go at once; an' how it suited her very well to leave as she was goin' off anyway, as her husband had made all preparations to start for America. Then by degrees we came round to the night when the diamonds were stolen.

"'It was wonderfully, cleverly done,' she said; 'an' no one has an idea of who did it, an' I'm thinkin' they'll never find out.'

"'Indeed it was cleverly done,' I replied; 'but there's mighty smart detectives goin' about in London, an' Sir Henry has any amount watchin' for the guilty parties.'

"'Do you say so, now?' she cried, and I I thought she grew a trifle paler; 'but it's not likely they'd stay in the country.'

"'No,' says I, 'they're sure to go to America.'

"'Dear, dear, do you think so,' she said, as quietly as possible, but her mouth twitched a bit; and she moved uneasily about on her seat.

"'Yes,' says I, 'an' isn't it a pity you wouldn't just give me a helpin' hand, Mary Ann?'

" ' Me,' she cried, growin' as red as a peony.
' What do I know about them ?'

" ' Well, maybe not much,' said I, carelessly.
' But you know this much — you know that
Master Hugh Brown never touched them dia-
monds.'

" ' Of course he didn't. Master Hugh's a
gentleman, every inch of him ; besides he wasn't
in the house.'

" ' No,' said I, ' of course he wasn't ; but
there's others that was, an' if you happen to
have an idea of who they are, if you'd just drop
them a hint, that supposin' they'd pawned the
jewels, it would be a good thing for them to
send the tickets to Sir Henry Randall, or even
to me ; for,' says I, givin' her a wink ' I've my
ideas strong upon the subject, an' think I know
who the parties are.   If those tickets were sent
to him some day, Sir Henry would let the
robbers go, I'm perfectly sure and certain, for
the sake of his invalid son, who would have to
give evidence in the case, and might be injured
thereby.   But if it so happens that the thieves
go on board, without havin' given up the
tickets or the diamonds, they'll find the detectives looking through their boxes, an' that
might be awkward, to say the least of it.'

"'So it might,' she said, growin' very fidgety, an' openin' an' shuttin' a little bag she held in her hand. 'But it isn't likely they'll have either diamonds or tickets in their boxes. Thieves is generally pretty sharp. Ah, my goodness save us all. What is that?'

"An' before I had time to answer a word, there came a great bump, a terrific shock, an' Mary Ann was sent flyin' to one side of the carriage, an' I was sent flyin' to the other. For a minute, I was stunned like. But then I gathered myself up, an' went over to poor Mary Ann, who was lyin' all in a heap, her head against the seat.

"'Any one hurt in here?' asked a guard, lookin' in at the window.

"'This poor woman is in a faintin' fit,' I answered. 'Has there been an accident?'

"'Oh, nothin' much,' says he, gayly. 'There's nobody really the worse. We're close to the station, but the line's blocked, so we may be here for half-an-hour or so. If your friend is hurt may be it would be better to take her home in a cab.'

"'She wants air anyway, I think, so I'll just get her out of this for awhile,' said I, for I thought I'd like to keep Mary Ann, an' look after her a bit if she was hurt. The guard gave me a helpin' hand for she was quite insensible, an' carryin' her on to the side of the road we laid her down. In a few minutes she opened her eyes, and stared about her in surprise.

"'Where am I,' she cried, 'where am I? Old man, what have you brought me here for?'

"'Just for a little air,' I said. 'There was an accident, an' you fainted. The train cannot go on for some time, so I thought it better to bring you out here. We're close to Victoria, an' '—

"'An accident—the train late—good gracious, I'll miss him,' she cried, starting to her feet. 'But I'm very weak,' and puttin' her hand to her head she sat down again. 'Mr. Bradley,' she said, faintly, ' will you go back to the train, and look for my band-box that's under the seat, it's very valuable, and '—

"'Yes, yes, I'll get it for you,' I cried thinkin' maybe there was somethin' real precious in it."

"The bracelet, perhaps?" suggested Percy.

"No, no; I wasn't quite so green as that, Master Percy. However, whatever, I thought, off I started, found our carriage after some huntin' up an' down, an' looked under every seat an' in every corner, but there was no band-box to be found, nothin' but a greasy-lookin' envelope, with a big red seal on it.

"'The poor creature will be disappointed,' I said, 'for may be her best bonnet was in that box — it must have tumbled out of the train, or been picked up by'—

"''Halloa,' cried the guard; 'here's a glass of water for your friend. Is she in the train again?'

"''Not she,' said I, 'she was too weak to move. She's lyin' over there, where we put her just now.'

"''Not a bit of her. She's gone,' he answered. 'I took the water over for her, but she was not there to drink it.'

"''Not there, not there,' I cried, an' off I ran to look for her.

"'But he was quite right; Mary Ann had disappeared; not a trace of her was to be seen.''

"'What a pity,'' cried Percy. "'Could you not have run after her?''

"'I'm not much of a runner, Master Percy, an' if I was, I did not know where to run. So I just stood scratchin' my head, an' not knowin' what to do except to call myself names, an' that I did pretty smartly.''

"But the greasy envelope with the red seal?" said Sir Henry. "What about that?"

"Ah," said Joe, smiling, and bringing out a packet from his coat pocket. "There was somethin' in that to console me for the loss of my Mary Ann. The band-box was a ruse, Sir Henry, to get me out of sight; but the poor creature had taken my hint and left me this — or may be she had dropped it in mistake."

"But what is in it, Joe?" cried Percy. "What is in it?"

"Nothing more nor less than the two pawn-tickets, Master Percy, an' there they are!"

"That is capital," said Sir Henry, taking them from the old man's hand. "And I am very grateful to you for all the trouble you have taken. You have done more for us than all my paid detectives."

"Because my heart was in it, Sir Henry, because my heart was in it," cried Joe. "But what will you do now? Will you try to stop the thieves on their way to America, or will you be content with gettin' back the diamonds?"

"I shall let them go," said Sir Henry, promptly. "To prosecute them would cause us all too much pain. I will redeem the diamonds at once."

"Redeem the diamonds? What do you mean?" cried Percy. "Please, please, tell me what you mean?"

"My dear boy," said his father, "these little bits of pasteboard are pawn-tickets, given to the persons who pawned your aunt's jewels. By presenting these, and paying a certain sum of money, how much I cannot tell, we can buy the diamonds back, and take them away when we like."

"Really, really! Oh, Joe, you are a brick," and in a whirl of excitement, Percy sprang from the sofa, and threw his arms round the old man's neck.

"I'm right glad to have served you, Master Percy. I'd do anything for you an' your dear father, for you've been good an' lovin' to them that was good to me. It was the thought of clearin' Master Hugh, an' pleasin' his dear mother, that drove me on to watch Mary Ann. Still, I'm glad to have served you. An' now, Sir Henry, what about the diamonds? Will you go about them yourself, or send some one?"

"I will go myself this very night, Joe," cried Sir Henry. "Pawn-shops keep open late, I know, so I'll go off at once. The bracelet, I see, has been disposed of in the Strand — the star somewhere in the East End. I will get them, if possible, this evening, and take them to my sister immediately."

" Oh, papa, papa, let me go to Brighton with you," cried Percy. " Let me take back the diamonds to Aunt Lydia."

" Yes, Percy, most certainly you may. But do you think you could go to Brighton to-morrow? It is a long journey, remember."

" Not so very long — only an hour," cried the boy, eagerly. " I feel so well to-night; joy has given me fresh strength."

" I am glad to hear that," said his father, kissing him. " But I am afraid, when the excitement is over, you will feel knocked up."

" No, no, papa — indeed, I shan't."

" Well, I'll tell you what I shall do, Percy. I will go off now and look after these jewels; then, on Monday, I will take them to Brighton. You may come with me, but on one condition."

" What is it, papa?"

" That you keep very quiet all day to-morrow, and do not excite yourself in anyway."

" Very well, I promise," cried Percy, gayly.

"Hugh and I will go to church together, and we shall thank God for His great goodness to us all."

"Yes, Percy; but will that not be too fatiguing for you?" asked Hugh.

"No, dear, it will do me good," answered Percy, gravely. "I have many blessings to thank God for now."

"Yes, indeed, you have," said Hugh. "And if my mother thinks you strong enough"—

"Aunt Lucy said she thought I might safely go to-morrow; and I am going to have such a happy day. Little Susie is coming to see me, and you must all have afternoon tea in my room. Then, on Monday, Hugh, we shall start for Brighton. How delightful! You must come, too, you know; because Aunt Lydia must forgive us together. She must forgive me for being so wicked—and you—well, for being so good and charming," and Percy laughed merrily.

"Now, my dear boy, if you think of going to church to-morrow, and to Brighton on Monday," said his father, seriously, "you must really lie down and rest. I am quite nervous about you, you seem so feverish and excited."

"But, papa dear, it is only because I am so happy," cried Percy, with glowing cheeks.

"I am glad to hear that, my child. But you must try and rest. I will get Theo to come and sit beside you, whilst Hugh and I go off with Joe to see about the diamonds."

"Yes, that will be nice. But here comes Theo, just in the nick of time. Oh, what fun! She has not heard a word, so I shall be able to tell her the whole story myself. Come along, Theo, dear, and we'll have such a jolly talk."

"Papa," said the little girl, as she tripped up to her father, holding an orange-colored envelope in her hand, " here is a telegram for you. I wonder if it's anything about the diamonds."

"Mary Ann telegraphing to send us her address, perhaps," said Hugh, laughing.

"Very likely, you old stupid," cried Percy, giving his cousin a push. " But away you go, and get the bracelet and star for me."

"My dear Percy," said Sir Henry, sadly, as he glanced over the telegram, " we need not go to Brighton; your Aunt Lydia has gone to the North. Mr. Torrens has had some kind of a stroke, and she has gone off to take care of him."

"I am very sorry to hear it," said Percy. "Poor old man, I hope he will soon get better; but what shalt we do about the diamonds, papa?"

"We must send them after her, dear. That is all we can do now. It would be impossible to go North with them. I could not leave home at present."

"What a pity? Now I shall not be able to beg her pardon properly," said Percy. "I had planned it all so nicely."

"Well, it can't be helped, dear," replied his father. "You must write her a little note, and send it with the diamonds. The sight of them will, probably, soften her heart towards you."

"Did the policeman catch the thieves, papa?" asked Theo. "Are they locked up in prison?"

"No, dear; we have not been able to catch the thieves," said Sir Henry. "They are gone; but we shall soon get the diamonds; so, I am quite satisfied. Tell Theo the story, Percy, for I must go off with Joe and try and find where these pawn shops are. Good-night. You must not sit up too late. But I may trust your Aunt Lucy to send you to bed in good time. Good-night."

"Good-night, papa; good-night Joe," cried Percy and Theo in a breath.

"Good-night, dear children," said the old man. "May God keep and protect you," and then he turned away and followed Sir Henry from the room.

"Isn't he a splendid old chap?" asked Percy, as the door closed upon his friend. "He would go through fire and water to do a good turn for any one, I believe."

"Would he?" said Theo, doubtfully; "but please, Percy, tell me what he has done; you all seem greatly excited about something, but I haven't the faintest idea what it is."

"So much the better, my dear girl, and if you have a little patience you shall soon hear all particulars. I'm so glad you were not in the room when the old soul told us the story; for then I should not have the fun of telling it to you."

And, delighted at having such an eager listener, Percy poured forth the whole account of Joe Bradley's journey from Brighton, and the strange manner in which he had found the pawn tickets.

CHAPTER XIX.

FORGIVEN.

AND so, at last, the diamonds were re-covered, and, to Percy's delight, were packed off to his Aunt Lydia, accompanied by a note, in which he made a most humble apology for his past conduct, and implored her to write, and tell him that he was forgiven.

But Mrs. Torrens took not the slightest notice of this appeal, and merely acknowledged the receipt of the jewels in a short letter to her brother.

Percy was in despair at this cruel treatment, and in a burst of rage against his aunt, declared that he was sorry he had ever begged her pardon at all; and if he had known she was going to be so disagreeable, he would never have taken the trouble to hunt for her diamonds as he had done.

"But, Percy dear," said Hugh, gently; "I

thought you were anxious to repair the mischief that you had done. I thought you were sorry for your conduct, and wished to atone for it, not so much because it annoyed your Aunt Lydia, as because it was wicked, and offended God, who has been so good to you."

"Oh, yes, yes, Hugh; but how hard it is to remember that always. You are right, though; I am sorry for acting those lies because my conduct offended God; and I know—I feel that I well deserve some punishment; papa has been too good to me, too gentle and forgiving, and I have grown to expect every one to be the same."

"And as there are very few so kind and true, you must not hope that they will treat you as he has done. And, now, Percy, I am going to give you a little advice."

"What, more advice?" cried Percy, laughing. "It seems to me you keep an unlimited supply of that commodity about you; but it is generally good, I must confess. So let me hear what it is, please."

"I am sorry if I have given you too much," replied Hugh, gravely. "But if you will only follow my advice now, Percy, old man, I promise that I shall not give you any more for a very long time."

"Well, then, what is this extraordinary piece of wisdom, most sage adviser? I am impatient to know what I am to do. Am I to don sackcloth and ashes and do penance for my sins, until Aunt Lydia deigns to forgive me?"

"Not at all—quite the contrary. What I would advise you to do is this: Cultivate cheerfulness; forget Aunt Lydia; forget the diamonds; forget yourself; and try to be as happy as you possibly can."

"But, my dear Hugh"—

"But, my dear Percy," said Hugh, kindly, "believe me, that is the right thing to do. You mope too much. You nurse your sorrow and grievances; and, by doing so, you make your father unhappy."

"Oh, Hugh!"

"Yes, it is true. He watches you night, noon, and morning, and when he sees you moping about and hears you sighing, he is most unhappy and"—

"Hugh, I will take your advice. I would do anything to please my father; for oh, how

good, how tender he has been to me. For his
sake, then, I will try to be cheerful."

"That is right, Percy; and now I tell you
what we shall do. We will say a little prayer
every day, that Mrs. Torrens may soon forgive
you. But, except for that, we shall forget all
about her, and be as happy as possible."

"Yes, Hugh; and I will say that prayer
from the bottom of my heart. And oh, if you
only knew how grateful I am to God, for having sent me a friend like you. He alone knows
how much you have helped me, and how you
will still help me to overcome my wicked
temper and bad"—

"Hush, Percy; you have helped yourself,
dear. God knows how difficult it is for you to
be good. But He saw you were trying hard
to serve Him well, and so He helped you to
become good and gentle."

"Yes, I think He has helped me, and I
thank Him for doing so. But, Hugh, one of
the helps God sent me was you yourself, my
little friend."

"Very well; perhaps He did send me—
indeed I am sure He did. And oh, Percy,
what would have become of my mother—of

wee Susie, if I had not found Uncle Henry's pocket-book?"

"God alone knows that, Hugh, dear. But I am so glad, so glad that you did."

"And I thank God on my knees every day for His wonderful goodness in allowing me to find it."

"How solemn you look, to be sure," cried Sir Henry, coming into the room at this moment. "I never saw a pair of boys look so serious."

"Do we really, papa?" said Percy, looking up brightly into his father's face. "And yet we have just been saying how happy we are, and how jolly we are going to be from this day forward. I am going to get strong and"—

"I wish you could, dear lad," replied Sir Henry, with a sigh. "And now, Percy, I have come to tell you something. The doctor says you must have change of air; so I have taken a house for a couple of months down at Maidenhead. Would you like that, do you think?"

"Like it! I'd love it, papa; and I'm sure the change would do me good."

"I trust it may; but I am glad you like the idea. The house will be ready next week, and your Aunt Lucy has promised to come and stay with us, and bring Susie with her. So we must be off as soon as we can."

"The very minute we can get into our new abode," said Percy, gayly. "Dear father, how good and kind you are. I wish I could do something to show you how truly grateful I am."

"Get strong, well and happy, Percy. That is all the gratitude I want or expect."

"And that you shall soon have, dear father. From this day I will do my best to grow strong and happy."

"And when you are that, then I shall be perfectly content, dear boy," said his father, with a loving kiss. "But I must leave you for the present. I have letters to write in time for the post," and he went away to the library.

And Percy kept his promise. He tried hard to put Hugh's advice in practice, and was so far successful, that in a short time, every one remarked the change that had taken place in his health and spirits.

Theo said it was all due to the fresh country air that they enjoyed, since they had taken up their abode in the beautiful house by the river.

And in this Sir Henry agreed with her; for it seemed to him that the boy had visibly improved from the very hour that they had left Holland Park, and all its unpleasant associations.

But Hugh knew that change of air, though it had done much for Percy, was not the only thing that had made him so good and bright. He knew how the boy had fought and struggled; he knew how fervently he had prayed; and he thanked God for the grace He had bestowed on his cousin, and begged Him to give him strength to persevere.

Nevertheless, the change from London to the country had done Percy and his companions a great deal of good, and the long summer days flew rapidly by in the quiet seclusion of beautiful Fernside.

Mr. Barker, who had long since forgiven Percy his insolence, came down from town every day, and the boys worked well and steadily at their lessons all the morning. Then, when he had taken his departure, the afternoons were given up to boating and tennis, which occupations they all found most entertaining.

"I don't think I was ever so happy in my

life before," cried Theo, one day, as she and the two boys strolled up the lawn, and seated themselves upon the grass. " This place is so lovely; the weather is so fine, and everybody so kind, that it is positively enchanting. Are these your sentiments, my friends?"

" Yes; they are mine, most certainly," answered Hugh, readily. " It is a delightful time and a charming abode. Don't you agree, Percy?"

" Yes—I do," said Percy, slowly; " but—I"—

" Now, no *buts*, dear boy," cried Theo, gayly. " I am sure you have been very happy since we came here—just six weeks to-day. And you have been so good and gentle."

" Thank you, Theo dear. I'm glad you think that; and I am happy—very happy. It was stupid of me to use the word *but*, if it made you think that I meant to say I was not; for I am extremely so, and much stronger than I ever was in my life before—far happier than I deserve to be. You are all so good—far too good to me."

" Now, I call that rubbish, Percy. No one could be too good to you," cried Theo. " I know you have been happy for a long time, for it is easily seen; but I just wanted to hear you acknowledge it. And now, I tell you what I'll do. It would be lovely to have our tea out here, so I'll run in and ask Grey to bring it out to us. Won't that be capital?"

"Delightful," cried Hugh. "But let me go and give Grey your message, Theo."

"No, no; you just stay where you are. I want to put on my tennis shoes. We'll have a splendid game after tea, Hugh, and you'll see what a beating I'll give you." And, kissing her hand the little girl tripped off, singing merrily as she went.

"Hugh," said Percy, gravely, as Theo disappeared, "have I managed to put your last piece of advice in practice, do you think?"

"Yes, indeed, you have, Percy. I never saw any one change so much as you have done within the last two months. My mother was delighted with you. She said you would grow up to be as good as Uncle Henry."

"Oh, Hugh," cried Percy, blushing brightly.

"She did, indeed. She is so fond of you. But I tell you what, Percy, you have surely had your reward for any trouble you may have had. Just think how happy dear Uncle Henry is. Why, I declare he seems to grow younger every day."

"Dear old father! I am glad I have managed to cheer up a bit for his sake, more than anything else. But, Hugh "—

"Yes, Percy."

"I have been saying that little prayer every day, and yet Aunt Lydia has never shown the slightest sign of forgiving me. I never thought she could have held out so long."

"But, Mr. Torrens has been ill, old chap, and "—

"Yes; that is true. But still, oh, I wonder if that prayer will ever be granted, Hugh. I feel so sorry for Aunt Lydia now, and I'd like to tell her so."

"I am quite certain your prayer will be granted some day, Percy. All prayers are. Perhaps it may not come just yet; but you must be patient and pray every day."

"Yes, indeed, I will," said Percy, earnestly. "But, Hugh, isn't that papa coming down the steps? Oh, dear, and he has a strange lady with him. How provoking! Now our nice little tea will be spoiled. I wonder where Theo is? She's very long giving her orders."

"Percy," cried Hugh, laying his hand upon

his cousin's arm. "Prepare yourself, dear boy. That lady is — is "—

"Who?" said Percy looking up sharply at the approaching visitor. "I declare it is, can it be? Yes, it is, really Aunt Lydia;" and flushing hotly he hurried across the lawn to meet Mrs. Torrens, who at that moment came down the steps into the garden.

"Aunt Lydia, I am very sorry," he cried, nervously. "I hope you will forgive me for my wicked conduct. Oh, have you come to say you have forgiven me?"

"Yes, dear, dear boy," she answered softly, and putting her arm round him she kissed him on the forehead. "I have forgiven you, and you must forgive me, Percy, for any unkindness that I may have shown to you; from this day you and I shall be friends."

"Oh, Aunt Lydia," was all Percy could say; but he looked up with a smile into his father's face.

"The poor lad has pined for your forgiveness, Lydia," said Sir Henry. "And he found it hard to make himself happy without it."

"I forgave you long ago, Percy; but I was so much taken up with my poor husband that I could not manage to come to you any sooner. I thought it better to come than to write."

"Yes; so it was," said her nephew. "I hope uncle is quite well, now."

"No; he is not quite well yet, Percy," she said, with a sigh; "and I fear it will be a long time before he is. We are starting for Melbourne in a few days. The doctors say a long sea voyage is the only chance for him."

"What a dreadful way to go, right off to Australia, Aunt Lydia," cried Theo, running up to greet the visitor. "Won't you be very sea-sick?"

"I dare say I shall, Theo, dear; but still if the voyage does my poor invalid good, I shall not complain. He is very hopeful himself, and quite anxious to be off."

"But won't you stay with us for a little while, Aunt Lydia?" said Percy. "Do stay, please, as long as you can!"

"Thank you, Percy. I will stay for a few days, if you care to have me. My sister-in-law is with your uncle, so I am not uneasy about him at present. But is that your cousin Hugh over there?"

"Yes, that is Hugh; the best boy that ever

lived," cried Percy. "And oh, Aunt Lydia, please speak kindly to him."

"Of course I will," she answered; "for I am afraid I treated him very badly. You are surprised to hear me speak so gently, Henry," she said, glancing at her brother with a smile. "But these last two months in my husband's sick room have taught me much, and made me grieve over many things that I have said and done during my life. Bring Hugh here, Percy."

"My dear Lydia," said Sir Henry, as his son went in search of his cousin, who had wandered away by himself, "your words and manner make me very happy and deeply grateful."

"Indeed? Then I am thankful that I came here to-day," she said, softly; "for I owe you much, dear brother—more than I can ever repay you;" and there were tears in her eyes as she spoke.

"Nonsense, Lydia," he answered hastily. "I only did what every brother ought to do—helped my sister when she wanted a little help. I only did my duty."

"Nevertheless, dear brother, you did it nobly, generously; and your conduct has touched and softened me, Henry, and made me ashamed of my pride and harshness in dealing with your son."

"All that is forgotten and forgiven now," he said, as he pressed her hand affectionately. "Do not mention it again."

Then Hugh was brought forward, blushing and trembling; but Mrs. Torrens looked at him so kindly, and spoke so gently, that she put him at his ease immediately.

"I treated you badly, Hugh, and I apologize. I thought my brother was too quick in acknowledging you as his nephew, and I felt certain he had been imposed upon. Now I know he was perfectly right, and had good reasons for all he did. I should very much like to meet your mother."

"You are very kind," said Hugh. "My mother is at Richmond."

"But she is coming to spend Sunday here," said Percy; "so then you shall see her. Aunt Lucy is the sweetest, kindest of aunties; and as for Susie — well, she is a darling."

"I should be really glad that you should meet Lucy," said Sir Henry. "She has suffered much during her life, but now she is peaceful and happy. She has been a great comfort to us all during Percy's long illness."

"Yes; so I heard," said Mrs. Torrens. "And now, Hugh, I hope you have forgiven me."

"Oh, Mrs. Torrens," cried Hugh, "I— had nothing to forgive."

"Yes, you had. I accused you of theft— most wickedly and unjustly. But I really believed that Mary Ann was a trustworthy servant; and as Percy said there were no robbers, I thought some one who knew the house must have taken the diamonds, and I fancied it was you. However, I am glad I was wrong. I am sure it is pleasant for Percy to have such a bright companion, and that you will always be good to him, and grateful to your kind benefactor and uncle."

"Most certainly I shall — always," said Hugh, firmly. "There is not much danger of my failing in either love or gratitude to my dear cousin and uncle."

"That is right. And now, Henry, I must tell you that Mary Ann and her wretched husband — the man who had the star at the inn, Percy — were caught in Liverpool the very day they were to have sailed for America, and have been sentenced to several years' penal servitude for some theft, committed I know not when nor how. But I am very glad; for it would have been terrible to think of such wicked creatures getting off without punishment."

"Yes; it certainly would," said Sir Henry. "Yet, I could not bring myself to prosecute them on account of the diamonds. It would have been very painful for us all, but especially for Percy."

"So it would," answered Mrs. Torrens, gently; "but I trust that Percy has had a lesson; and that no matter how disagreeable a person may be to him, he will never again try to be revenged."

"Never, indeed, aunt, never," said Percy, earnestly; "I have suffered too much in every way ever to think of doing such a thing again."

"I am quite sure of that," remarked his father; "my little lad has grown brave and good within the last few months; he now knows what it means to bear and forbear."

"Yes, father, I hope I do," whispered Percy; "but please don't praise me too much."

"I will not, dear boy; and now, my friends, let us talk of something else; let this conversation be the very last we shall ever hear of Percy's revenge."

"Very well, papa dear; so it shall," cried Theo, gayly; "so come along to tea; Grey has set it out so nicely in the little arbor down by the river."

"That will be charming, dear," replied Sir Henry; and offering his arm to his sister he led her away.

"Are there any more *buts* now to your happiness, Master Percy?" asked Theo, saucily.

"Not one, you old darling," he answered, brightly; "I feel as if I could never, never be unhappy again;" and throwing his arms around the little girl's neck he gave her a loving kiss.

"Come, Hugh, dear friend," he said, turning to his cousin, "let us join the tea-party in the arbor, and let us be as merry as merry can be."

Then with one hand in Theo's and the other in Hugh's, Percy danced down the garden after his father and aunt.

.　　.　　.　　.　　.

Mrs. Torrens remained at Fernside for a week; and, during that time, Percy did all he could to show her how much he had changed since her last visit to Holland Park. And, indeed, the children vied with each other in making her happy during her stay amongst them.

This delighted Mrs. Torrens, and she told

Sir Henry that they were the nicest little creatures she had ever known; that the week of quiet happiness spent in their society had done her good, and strengthened her for her sea journey.

And when at last she took her departure, the farewells were long and affectionate; for the children, whose enemy she had been in former times, had learned to love her, and were sorry to see her go.

And so this visit did a great deal of good; and when it was over, Percy returned to his various occupations, feeling more content than he had ever done in his life.

And thus we leave our young friends as happy as it is possible for children to be; surrounded by every luxury, yet not carried away by an undue love of the good things of this world; deeply impressed by the goodness of God towards them, and determined to work bravely, and become truly virtuous.

And to those of my readers who are interested in the future of these little people I will say, that as time went on their efforts were crowned with success.

Percy grew up to be a noble fellow, full of talent and generosity; whilst Hugh distinguished himself in every way, and became the pride of his kind benefactor and uncle, a true blessing to his widowed mother and little sister.

And Theo?　Well, Theo grew to be what it should be the aim and object of every girl to become, a gentle, kind-hearted woman.